<u>Aurora Knights</u>
Loyalties

By Robert Wiesehan

Robert Wiesehan lives in Missouri where relentless thoughts of fantasy and games regularly deprive him of much needed sleep. You can find more information on all of his creative projects by checking out his Twitter account.

www.twitter.com/RobertWiesehan

<u>My Heartfelt Thanks</u>

To God

To my parents and brother, for their encouragement

<u>To my feedback readers</u>
Emily Wenstrom
Marilyn Wiesehan
Joshua Ahrens
Allison Parker

<u>To my editor</u>
Kristen House

<u>To my cover artist</u>
Hugh Rookwood

And to Ashley, because she insisted.

1

The last wisps of Ria's consciousness seeped back into her body from the Aurora Crystal. The process always unsettled her a little. It was like coming in out of the cold and warming up to find feeling returning to a limb you hadn't known you had.

The swirling lights and colors that danced just beyond her closed eyelids planted a headache just behind her brow, but she didn't have time to dwell on the pain. A field of magic as powerful as what she'd just sensed demanded swift action.

She gripped the sides of the cushioned metal frame that cradled her and pulled herself forward with a grunt, straining against the complaints of her aging joints. Soon she was seated upright before the hovering Aurora Crystal, shielding her eyes from the glow it gave off as they adapted to the light. Loud taps of hard-soled shoes echoed off of the stony floors and walls. No doubt the shrine maidens on duty had seen her and were rushing to her aid. Ria swung her legs out over the side of the bed and hurried to stand, but numbness still lingered. She felt her body begin to pitch forward.

"Oracle!" a young woman's voice called. Two pairs of hands caught her arms and shoulders, saving her from what would have been an unceremonious meeting with the floor.

Ria quietly cursed the steady march of time that had left her frail and submitted to her body's slow process of recovery. Once her vision cleared, she turned her eyes toward the broad, golden vault doors in front of which she'd rested for so many years.

Behind them lay the Aurora Arms, the five greatest weapons mankind had ever forged. She'd spent the better part of her life waiting for a sign that forces of chaos and darkness were on the rise again; a sign that called for her to open the vault and arm new heroes.

The sign had come. It was time to call new Aurora Knights.

She turned her attention back to the shrine maidens supporting her, each clad in a loose-fitting red and white habit. "Alert the king," Ria ordered the taller one. "Tell him I will see him within the hour. And tell him it will not wait!" The maiden nodded and tip-tapped quickly out of the room.

The remaining maiden, a small, nervous looking one wearing glasses, tucked herself under Ria's arm to support her fully. "What do you need me to do, Oracle?" she asked.

"Take me down to the dining room, then go fetch some of the other girls to help you. I'll need a light meal and my dress vestments. Send others up here and remove the bed from this chamber. I won't be sleeping before the Crystal for the foreseeable future."

"Yes, Oracle."

As they crossed the room, Ria took stock of its state for the first time in a season. Numerous tidy shelves filled with books of ancient lore lined the walls of the room, and writing quills and study aids sat arranged beneath magelamps on the sturdy wooden tables. Good, she thought. Her maidens had been vigilant even about the little details during her slumber. That was promising.

Satisfied, she proceeded to the next room, still supported by her attending shrine maiden. Together they stepped onto the massive golden disc set into the floor. "Dining room," the young shrine maiden commanded it, and it slowly carried them down the shaft at the center of Aurora Tower.

There was no sense in just preserving awkward silence as they rode down to the lower floors. "I don't think I've seen you before, sister," Ria said. "I'm afraid I don't usually get the opportunity to get to know my shrine maidens with all of the time I spend scrying. What is your name?"

"I'm Charise, Oracle," the girl replied.

"Have you been a shrine maiden long?"

"Only for about a year now. It's just the first time I've been on watch at a time you awakened."

Ria nodded. "And why did you join us, Charise?

The young shrine maiden hesitated. Though she still supported the Oracle with one arm, Charise fidgeted with the hem of her red and white habit with her free hand. She looked away, watching the tower's middle floors slip past them.

Ria pursed her lips and nodded. Other shrine maidens had responded like this to her questioning before. "Let me guess, you joined for the education and training we provide, expecting that I wouldn't call a group of Knights during your service?"

"M-maybe, Oracle." She lowered her head, refusing eye contact.

Ria pursed her lips. The girl's motivation was more common among the maidens than she liked to admit. The Knights were mobilized infrequently, and in times of peace, serving at Aurora Tower gave many young women access to education and training otherwise outside of their means.

Still, now was the time to make sure the girl had the will to carry on. "I'm afraid that gamble hasn't paid off for you. So, what now? We'll have no use for a maiden without tenacity when things get tough. Should I expect you hesitate like this when I give you orders to support our Knights?"

"What? No, Oracle!" Charise stammered. "No, I won't let you down."

The girl had a ways to go for sure, but, Ria reminded herself, she too had joined the shrine maidens with a few rough edges. "Good. Self-doubt is only human, Charise, but your Knights and sisters need to be able to depend on you. Your work may take place behind the scenes, but it's no less critical to keeping the world safe."

Charise nodded. Though she still nibbled at her lower lip in her silence, she met Ria's gaze more easily now.

The disc that carried them slowed to a gentle stop near the bottom of the tower. The two stepped off and went to prepare Ria to brief King Magnus Vatri.

XXX

Ria awaited the king in a private meeting chamber within the castle proper. His servants had delivered tea, fruit, and assurances that King Vatri was on his way, but none of it was of any use to the Oracle. The refreshments sat untouched on the ornate wooden table, and the assurances did nothing to ease her certainty that the king was sending her a message by making her wait.

I am more important than you are. We will meet when I am ready.

They had done this dance nearly every time the Oracle had woken from her season-long slumbers to report suspicious phenomena that might threaten the world. She would arrive prepared to present her findings from a season spent scrying on various regions all over the world, and he would come in late with an insincere apology at the ready. She'd deliver a detailed report, and the lout would yawn conspicuously. She'd finish with a recommended plan of action, and he'd oversimplify the whole report. "Nothing of concern, then?" he'd say. "Good. Enjoy your nap then. I'll see you in three months."

It was a shame she had no choice but to tolerate the man. The shard of the Aurora Crystal that had been bound to the Vatri family a thousand years ago was one of two keys needed to open the vault at the top of Aurora Tower. It couldn't just be yanked out of King Magnus' hands and used without the blessing of a Vatri.

The other shard hung from a simple cord around her own neck. She ran her fingers over it reflexively as she silently cursed Oracle Presca's lack of foresight. Unlike King Magnus, King Tragar of Vatrisland had been a great friend to the first Oracle of the Arms, and the two had forged a close alliance. In exchange for the king's invitation to build Aurora Tower within the protective walls surrounding his castle at Cloudbreach, she'd agreed to address the fears of many that a group of Aurora Knights might someday be called to use their incredible power to bully nations that questioned an Oracle.

Presca had bound the second shard of the Aurora Crystal to the Vatri family bloodline. Her measure had ensured that no future Oracle would be able to open the Tower's vault and assemble a team of Knights without first hearing an outsider's perspective.

In that age, the plan had made sense. Kingdoms of men had been fewer and farther between back then, and terrifying creatures and tyrannical warlords had rampaged across the world unchecked. People of different regions assumed the best of one another and worked together to survive against greater threats.

Things were different today. Civilization had sprawled out to fill precise, carefully guarded borders. Rulers viewed one another with suspicion and rarely cooperated without a web of deals and contracts codifying every last word of their negotiations. In this world, Oracle Presca's choice to locate Aurora Tower in the political heart of Vatrisland left Ria's maidens struggling to maintain their image as an unbiased order that held the whole world's best interests above those of Vatrisland.

Vatrisland's people didn't make it any easier for the Aurora Knights and their maidens to appear independent. The nation's culture had shaped itself around being the home of the Aurora Arms. Children were raised on tales of heroic valor, and many grew up to volunteer to serve its military. Even the poorest one-room schools in the sprawling kingdom managed to afford to pay local militiamen to teach their students basic combat training.

Their great national pride at being the home of the Aurora Knights fostered an unhealthy sense of ownership over the Arms. Each of the thirteen times in the past thousand years that a team of Knights had been assembled to drive back darkness, the reality of the weapons' location had almost always ensured that most of the five were natives of the mountainous kingdom. Conflicts sometimes arose when Knights were forced to choose between the good of their country and the greater good of all people.

Ria's stomach churned with anxiety as she considered all of the factors that complicated her calling. She had to put her mind at ease before King Vatri arrived. Winding herself up with worry would only make it harder for her to present her findings and make her request effectively.

She tried to focus on the sensations of being awake and back in her body instead. She turned her open palms to the softly crackling fireplace beside her and smiled as its warmth crept into her skin. The dancing flames glinted off the gold accents on her red and white formal vestments. Once her fingers warmed, she ran them through her short gray hair a few times to make sure that the walk across the windy castle grounds hadn't left her looking disheveled as she gazed out of a nearby window. Night had fallen over Cloudbreach, the bustling mountainside capital of Vatrisland, and the enchanted magelamp orbs that lit the streets drew her eyes to the towering statues of past Aurora Knights that dotted the cityscape.

The moment of quiet she enjoyed didn't last long enough. The voices of boisterous men grew louder and louder as they approached the meeting room door. At last, a chuckling King Magnus Vatri pushed the door open and entered.

"And see what your wife thinks of that!" Magnus bellowed

out the door to someone Ria couldn't see. The voices from the hallway roared in laughter, no doubt at a lewd suggestion of some kind the king had just made as he bid farewell to his company. He turned his attention to the Oracle. "Ria, my dear! How's my favorite sour seer, hm?"

"King Vatri," she bowed her head slightly, resisting the urge to sigh. What a fine way to start off their meeting. The king shuffled into the room and flopped into one of the seats. He had a habit of declaring celebrations on short notice, and from the looks of things, he had just come from such an occasion. He wore fine purple garments adorned with jewels and precious metals. Beneath his graying blond beard, his face flushed bright red. Wonderful. He tended to be extra belligerent after a few drinks.

"So." The king clapped his mighty hands together with a loud crack. "What is it this time, hm? Same as always, I take it? Just your usual fidgety worrying over all of the little things? If so, I'll be happy to wrap this up quickly and get you back to sleep searching for spooky monsters and magical whatnots."

"I'm afraid not, your majesty." Ria remained composed, seating herself across from the drunken king. "Last time I awoke, the brief your scribe gave me mentioned that your army had been driven to a stalemate fighting undead controlled by a rather persistent necromancer in the Cryptwastes to the north. I made a point to focus my divinations on that region over the course of this past season, as a stalemate seemed out of character against the forces of a single necromancer."

"Ah, so you found more of them then? Crafty blighters! I'll see that—"

"No, your majesty," Ria interrupted. "That's the problem. There is only one necromancer there. No necromancer, even a phenomenally talented one, should have the capacity to bend to his will an undead army large enough and potent enough to halt your men. Near this spellcaster, on the other hand, I can detect enough

11

organized, risen dead to wipe out your entire force, and yet for some reason, he holds them back. I'm beginning to believe that he wants your men there for something."

The king sighed at her details. "And let me guess. You don't have a clue what that 'something' is, do you?"

Ria cringed. "No, your majesty, I don't. There seems to be a growing field deep within the wastes blocking my vision. I pressed against it with all of my will many times as I slept, but could not penetrate it."

The king rose from his seat and walked a few slow steps to an open window. He leaned against its frame, taking in a bit of fresh air. "So I'll double the contingent out there. Triple if you like. We've got the men for it. We'll break the standstill and have them home before the first leaf falls in autumn."

"I'm not sure you're considering the magnitude of the unknown that we're dealing with here, your majesty. This is very suspicious. We'd be better off mobilizing the Aurora Arms before this situation gets truly out of control. Miles of the Cryptwastes are suddenly impenetrable to my scrying, and defended by an undead army the likes of which we've never faced before. You and I both know what kinds of things are out there. Ancient tomb guardians, magical relics, and likely whatever caused the Blightfire that incinerated every living thing in the Itradi Empire. If you keep sending ordinary men out there, you'll be subjecting them to the schemes of a madman."

The king turned to the Oracle, his brows furrowed in a scowl. "Are you questioning my judgment, Oracle? That's a bold road to walk in my castle. You know well that tradition demands a king of Vatrisland has served in her military, and serve I have. I know well what my forces are capable of."

Ria backpedaled. She'd lose any chance to mobilize her Knights if he became hostile. "Your Majesty, I did not mean to—"

"What about you, hm?" he interrupted. "You've spent over

12

fifty years of your life watching the world pass you by in your magical slumber, and what have you to show for it? Season after season without a single catastrophe that ordinary men cannot handle without your Knights, and you're not the least bit eager to throw the vault open and justify all of that lost time? You're asking an awful lot based not on information, but anxious ignorance." He stopped for just a moment before snidely adding, "Not that I blame you; I might be bitter too were I in your shoes."

Ria closed her eyes briefly, trying to push his jab from her mind. She wished she could just let it go, but now he was under her skin. "King Vatri, it is not lost time. I gave that time willingly, and you know it. The day that Oracle Celeste told me that I was worthy of her mantle was the proudest day of my life. My family celebrated with me. They knew that what they lost in time spent with me, they'd gain in my vigilance over the world. They encouraged me, knowing that when the need arose, I would put their protectors to task."

"Come now, Oracle," Magnus cooed smugly, "Beneath all those robes and wrinkles, you're still as fallible as the rest of us. You've suffered all of the responsibility of your role and never enjoyed any of the power. Here you are in your twilight years and the temptation has finally cracked through your shell. Welcome to being human. We're pleased to have you."

That was enough. Ria stood and laid a hardened gaze upon him. "Magnus, I didn't suffer all of those dismissive meetings with you only to be told that I'm in error the one time I deem a threat to be suspicious enough to act upon. If you don't take this seriously now, not just Vatrisland, but the whole world could lose countless lives in the three months before I could be woken again. You know that my key, like yours, will only respond to its bound bearer's will!"

"That's a risk I'm willing to take! My forces will be sufficient!" he barked.

13

"How can you just ignore what I'm sensing?" She raised her voice to match his.

"I do not need your Knights or your assistance with this, Oracle!" he roared. "Vatrisland wields the most powerful army in the world. We are years ahead of our neighbors in integrating magic into our forces. Our spellblades are perfected to the point of mass production, and the head of my magecraft division refines her new magelock pistols further every day. Our prototype skyship is the largest flying vessel ever known. The age of the Aurora Knights is over! We needn't charge a few maverick heroes with the whole world's safety any longer!"

The room fell silent, save for the crackling of hot logs in the fireplace. Ria balled her hands into fists at the thought of being trapped in her unconscious state. In the near omniscience of her dreams, she would be forced to watch, helpless as every tragedy unfolded before her.

Was Magnus right? Though Vatrisland's army never fought off anything as strong as the kinds of evils that the Aurora Knights took down on their own, military cooperation between the other major nations could potentially make up the difference. It was an awful stretch though, to assume King Vatri wouldn't be arrogant to the point of souring an alliance with other leaders. He did not have a history of playing well with others.

And with an army that strong, if no one could assemble the Knights...

...he wouldn't have to.

"You're unopposed," she murmured.

The king had turned toward the window in the silence. He didn't turn to face her again. "Hm?"

"That's why you don't want the Knights assembled. If they're around, you lose the political leverage your army grants you. If other leaders defy you, you can make threats to bring them back into line. If they need to depend on you to protect them, you can demand generous terms for assistance. No other pair of armies together are a match for Vatrisland's, and even if they were to ally against you, the burden of coordinating their operations would render them less efficient than your unified force."

The king made no reply. Ria stepped closer to him, the answers tumbling out of her mouth as quickly as she could assemble them. "If the Aurora Knights are deployed, you're no longer the biggest dog in the yard. You'd risk their wrath if you threatened another realm unjustly. You are afraid, King Vatri. You're afraid that our world's sworn defenders will judge you, and that you'll be seen for the bully that you are."

Another silence fell over the room. The king still faced away from Ria, but his hesitation was all the answer she needed. A tyrant stood between her and the safety of the world. No doubt the first Knights were turning in their graves. This was how divided and distrustful the world had become.

"That is a heavy accusation to level at a king, Oracle," he finally answered, turning to face her with an emotionless stare. He walked toward her slowly. "Are you sure you can bear the weight of it?"

"You do not scare me," Ria spat back quietly, narrowing her eyes as he loomed over her. "Every leader on the continent supports the efforts of the Aurora Knights. You'd rally every last one of them against you in a heartbeat if you harmed me."

"Harm you?" he asked. "Please, Oracle. Paranoia doesn't become you. I have no intention of harming you. All I plan to do is deny your request."

Magnus strode past Ria to the door behind her and tugged it open, gesturing for her to leave.

Ria gaped at him. "Magnus, you—"

"Thank you for your report, Oracle, but I see no need to mobilize the Aurora Arms," he declared loudly, catching the attention of passing nobles. "You should probably get back to sleep soon. I'm told it takes you a week to settle into the absolute clarity of your trance. You have no time to waste."

Silence. The two stared one another down. Neither flinched, but Ria could feel her heart sinking in her chest. The seconds that passed seemed like minutes.

"What will it take to have your cooperation?" she offered.

"This is not negotiable."

"Don't give me that." Ria closed the gap between herself and the king, stepping right into his personal space. Though her full height only came up to Magnus' nose, she stood in his shadow, her eyes narrow, resolved. "You may be infuriatingly bull-headed, but your stubbornness would find its limit if the deal were sweet enough. Now, what will it take?"

Magnus pushed the door closed again, restoring their privacy. "Excite me, Oracle," he murmured through a slight grin. "Make me an offer."

She knew how this worked. Once he knew where she was willing to start, he could drag it further in his favor with a counter-proposal. Ria felt like prey. She mentally scolded herself for not having planned for something like this. He'd know she was grasping at straws if she hesitated. She forced herself to start her sentence without a clear idea of how she'd end it. "In absolute defiance of the long-respected traditions that have governed every commissioning of Aurora Knights until this day, you will be allowed to select a member to put on the team."

"Oh?" He raised his eyebrows.

Oh indeed. That and a number of other choice words best not said in polite company. She wished with every fiber of her being that she hadn't opened her mouth, but it was too late now. She forced an air of confidence and nodded, "You may select the most blindly patriotic, completely loyal puppet in your command. Your proxy can parrot your will to the other Knights, and you'll be able to depend upon him or her to draw arms in your name should

16

Vatrisland's fate be put at stake against the fate of another nation."

The king offered a predatory smile. "Not enough. He must be Knight-Captain."

The chaotic mix of anger and alarm was too much to contain. She answered through clenched teeth, doing what she could to show more of the former emotion than the latter. "You know that cannot be done. The leader of the Knights is the only member selected in advance. He's already aware of his role. The long notice he's given lets him prepare himself for the position, and scout far and wide for the finest warriors. He is given full power to invite or deny any other Knight into the fold."

"Exactly." The king moved in for the kill. "Leader. Take it or sleep."

She couldn't flinch. Not now. "Fine!" she spat.

The king broke into an open-mouthed smile with a scoff. "Fine?"

"Fine. If this is what it takes, I won't damn us all to spite you. The world needs the Knights, and we're better off with them tainted by your agenda than with no Knights at all. Pick your loyal dog. I'll deliver him the news myself."

King Vatri boomed in laughter, "A splendid idea! Just fantastic, Oracle! Head down into the city then and drop by The Victor's Chalice. Darius tends to make his way over there with his fellow soldiers around this time each week. You'll almost certainly find him there."

Ria stammered, wide-eyed. "Y-your son? He's going to lead them?" It was one thing to have someone with a bias commanding the Knights. It was another thing entirely to put the Prince of Vatrisland in control. How could she expect to sway Darius against his own father's will?

"Of course! Can't think of a better match. I'll finally be able to put the little scrapper to work on something of real value. Eager to please, too. He'll be perfect!"

17

The Oracle swallowed and placed a hand on the back of a chair to brace herself. What had she just agreed to? Had she just handed the most powerful heroes the world had ever known over to a tyrant? Nightmare scenarios played out in her head as she struggled to recompose herself.

"Too excited, Oracle? I know the feeling. Take your time. I'm sure he and his friends will be out late enjoying themselves. I look forward to cracking open that glorious vault with you tomorrow. It will be a proud day for the kingdom!" With that, King Vatri left the meeting room, swinging the door shut behind him.

Ria took several more minutes to herself in the meeting room. She couldn't panic now. The very calling of the Oracle and the Knights was to face the unthinkable, and she would not be so proud as to think that this was the worst any Oracle had ever faced. What was done was done. Damage control was the next step, and to do that, Ria needed to get to know the fiery prince she'd be dealing with.

Composed, and now with a plan of action, she exited the meeting room at a swift walk. Charise, who had still waited outside patiently in a nearby chair, now bolted upright and matched the Oracle's pace. "Miss Ria, how did the meeting go?"

"We have much to do, Charise. That old viper thinks he holds all of the cards, but he's got another thing coming if he thinks he can leash the Aurora Knights. Come, and pay attention. We'll figure out a way to turn this for good yet."

The two strode out of the castle into the cool night air, and down the mountainside road into the city. Far above them, the aurora danced in glorious display like a shimmering ribbon across the late evening sky, and Ria swore on it that she wasn't beaten yet.

2

Prince Darius Vatri wasn't the kind to back down from a challenge, be it in arm wrestling, sparring, or drinking. Considering that he'd already faced down challengers in the first two activities earlier today during drills with Vatrisland's military, it was only natural that he'd find himself squatted beneath a keg at The Victor's Chalice once again exercising his talent at the third. He and his friend, Bainon, plugged the spigots with their mouths as their fellow soldiers shouted and cheered each to outdrink the other.

The prince peered to one side, staring down his competition as best he could from the awkward angle. Bainon, a burly man with wild red dreadlocks, returned the look and upped the ante by jabbing him in the side with outstretched fingertips. Darius fought off the burning sensation in his throat and jabbed back. The onlookers cheered all the more. Their contest would end soon, one way or another.

Suddenly he saw his opportunity. Bainon braced against the counter and kicked at Darius' calf. Rather than try to swing his leg aside, he endured the kick, grabbed the extended leg, and gave it a mighty yank. Bainon toppled and spat beer as the keg's open spigot leaked into his eyes.

"He beat Bainon! He got 'im!"

The men roared their approval at Darius. When he could swallow no more, he fell back from his squatting position beneath the keg, spraying the remaining contents of his mouth out in a boisterous laugh. Beer splattered his shirt and vest, and more droplets clung to his short blond hair and goatee. The men hauled Darius to his feet and he shuffled out of the crowd, snatching another full tankard from the bar, to search for a seat and let another soldier try his luck beneath the kegs.

The bar's features swam in his vision as he wove his way through the clusters of joyful patrons. It brimmed with the style of old Vatrisland. Sturdy stone walls extended up into the darkness to meet with the timbers of a steeply sloped roof that shed winter snows easily. Half a dozen fireplaces scattered throughout the broad common room blazed with incensed logs, filling the room with a sweetness that masked the sweaty funk of relaxing laborers. Weapons and armor of past heroes hung high on the walls alongside paintings and busts of their bearers, safely out of reach of clumsy patrons. On a massive stone slab at the back, a trio of performers stirred some to dance with soaring folk songs played on lute, pipes, and drums. The bar throbbed with the vitality of its proud homeland, and Darius sighed contentedly, letting the atmosphere wash over him.

The prince flopped his tall, muscled frame into a cushioned armchair, stressing a loud creak of protest out of the seat and the floorboards beneath it. Bainon finished toweling beer out of his dreads and hustled over to Darius, accompanied by their friend Ottrick.

"You're gonna earn yourself a serious gut if you keep putting 'em back like that, Dar. And let me tell ya, I ain't gonna roll you on and off the battlefield if you do," said Ottrick with a sly grin.

"Hey," Darius shot back at the blond, lean soldier, smiling. "That's a funny thing to say to a guy whose coin you're drinking on. Trying to get yourself cut off?"

Ottrick chuckled, raising his hands in surrender. Bainon found a seat beside the prince and tossed the half-soaked towel into the prince's lap. "Don't mind Ottrick, Dar. He doesn't speak for all of us. I for one am happy to see the fruits of my taxes coming back to me in my mug."

"See? Eh?" Darius pointed at Ottrick. "Bainon knows who butters his bread."

The men laughed warmly. Darius was only two months into his compulsory military service, but he already felt perfectly at home with the men alongside whom he drilled. Though all nobility in Vatrisland received basic training with weaponry, Darius had gladly continued practicing long after he'd completed the minimum requirement, and now, even with his service just beginning, he could best most of his squad in duels.

It was all a welcome relief from what he'd seen of life in the royal court. The few experiences he'd had among the subtle and cunning politicians at the castle had always left him feeling anywhere from bored to disgusted. Bunch of silver-tongued manipulators. Soldiers were honest. If they liked you, they cheered. If they didn't, they told you with a gauntlet to the jaw. Simple.

He scowled and gritted his teeth. Every time he thought about how much he was enjoying his military service, he remembered why he was there in the first place. Less than two years from now, he'd have his compulsory service behind him. Far too soon, he'd be yanked out of this world that he understood to join a world of councils and envoys at his father's side. Long days of politicking and false smiles awaited him too soon.

"Hey, you still with us Dar?" Bainon asked, breaking him free from his grim reflection.

"Mm? Yeah, was just thinking." The men didn't reply, but just motioned Darius to continue. He went on. "You know we probably won't see a real battle for the next two years with me in the squad, right? I mean, we'll probably get deployed on a token engagement. Something small; a cleanup job so they can tell the

21

people that I fought. You won't see any monsters worth worry till I'm gone."

"Yeah, actually," Ottrick chimed in. "But somehow knowing that I wouldn't have anything trying to murder me for a few years didn't sour my mood. Guess I'm just funny like that."

Darius shook his head. "You know what I mean." He gestured to the inspiring art and arms that hung high on the walls, "Don't you want to be part of all this? Testing your might? Defending Vatrisland? Coming home to the cheers of her people?"

"Fighting undead terrors up north?" Ottrick added.

Bainon took a turn. "Choking on grit in a dust storm?"

"No women for months on end?"

"Eating tack every day?"

"Learning what your guts look like when someone cuts you right across the midd—?"

"Hey! I'm drinkin' here!" Bainon interrupted, slugging Ottrick on the arm.

"I know, I know. I'm not blind to that stuff, it's just that, in the end...." Darius trailed off as he swept his eyes across the walls of the room once more. Armored figures posed proudly in painted portraits, their gazes looking down upon him, daring him to aspire to greatness. He could hear the cheers of victory as he admired key turning points in battles long past depicted on canvas. Aurora Knights hovering mid-leap over a sinister enemy general or rampaging beast seemed to spring to life in his mind as he surveyed the art. Swords glittered like trophies, steel and crystalline blades shining in the dancing firelight, retired to a place of honor to inspire men just like him for generations to come.

"It's all worth it," he murmured.

"Uh, Dar?" Bainon gave the prince a light swat on the arm, bringing him back to his senses. The entire bar had fallen silent during his moments lost in thought. He turned, following the gazes of slack-jawed patrons to the front door of the bar. Their shock was

22

justified.

There, attended by a single shrine maiden shifting and fidgeting uncomfortably near the center of attention, stood the Oracle of the Arms. She looked much like she did in the statues and paintings that Darius had seen, if with a few more wrinkles near her eyes and dour, serious mouth, but he couldn't mistake her for another even in his state. Her presence commanded attention as she scanned the room, shoulders pulled back, searching the crowd like a bird of prey.

At last she settled her gaze upon Darius and walked toward him, her maiden shadowing her like a shy child hiding behind her mother's skirt when faced with a stranger. Darius reflexively stood as she closed the distance, and though at his impressive height he towered a full head's length over her now, it did nothing to favor him in the face of her palpable resolve. She studied the prince, grimacing in disapproval at his beer-stained shirt and flushed face.

Though she unnerved him, Darius spoke first. "May I...offer you a dr—?"

"No." She continued looking him over.

A long pause passed between the two. Darius cleared his throat, unaccustomed to feeling disadvantaged in an exchange, and tried again. "Can I help you, Oracle?"

She looked straight into his eyes and spoke with piercing sincerity. "Stars, I hope so. Say goodnight to your friends, Prince Vatri, and meet me outside. We have an urgent matter to discuss." The Oracle turned back toward the door and began walking out before adding, "And tell your commanding officer that you're being discharged from service effective immediately."

"Wait, what?" Darius looked to his friends for answers, but their baffled expressions matched his own. She couldn't take this away from him. She didn't have the power.

The prince handed his tankard off to Bainon and made for the door, pushing past the whispering and speculating patrons. In

23

moments he was out in the cool night air, eyes adjusting to the light of the magelamps on the street and the aurora high above. He scanned his surroundings and spotted the Oracle. She and her attendant had seated themselves at a bench beside a nearby fountain.

Darius hustled over to the women. She couldn't just rip him from the first position in which he'd ever felt at home. Oracle of the Arms or not, the old woman was about to get a piece of his mind. "Hey!" he barked. "How about you explain yourself? Last time I checked, you didn't have the authority to discharge anyone from the army; much less the prince of the damned kingdom."

"Oh, believe me, Prince Darius, if I'd had any way to keep you exactly where you were, rest assured I'd have done just that." The Oracle rose, meeting Darius with her own bitterness. "Unfortunately, it seems I'm being put to task in an age during which tradition is remarkably malleable."

"What are you talking about?"

The Oracle sighed. "Due to... unanticipated complications, as of tomorrow morning you will be commissioned as the leader of a new generation of Aurora Knights."

Darius scoffed. He hadn't figured the Oracle would be such a prankster. "Right. And what's the punchline?"

Ria shook her head. "This is no joke, Darius."

Was she really serious? He softened his demeanor slightly. "What about the chosen leader? He get himself killed or something?" Darius asked. He was no scholar, but one didn't make it to eighteen years old in Vatrisland without learning the traditions that governed the Aurora Knights. Even a schoolboy could tell you that somebody always got prepped in advance for the top spot.

"I'm afraid not. Rather, your father insisted you be given the position before he'd agree to mobilize the Arms."

Darius reeled for a moment. "M-my father? That doesn't make any sense." There had been a time, back when he'd been no more than six or seven years old, that he and his father had been close, but the passing of his mother had driven a rift between them. Magnus had condemned his gift for battle as "wasteful roughhousing" and an "obsession ill-suited for an heir to the throne."

But now, an Aurora Knight? Darius' disbelief gave way to excitement. "So, I'll be leader. I'll wield the Titangavel then?" He had seen the massive maul in paintings before, but never in person. The Aurora Arms had last left their vault decades before he was born. Now, he would bear the legendary hammer that granted superhuman strength and power over earth and stone. A grin spread itself uncontrollably onto his face.

"You'll have a lot of responsibility on your shoulders, Prince Vatri," the Oracle scolded him. "Innocent people the world over will be counting on you to protect them. Don't be so thrilled at the thought of power."

"No, no. It's not that. Well, maybe a little," Darius explained. "This is just unexpected. I didn't imagine father would give me this kind of opportunity to bring glory to Vatrisland."

"And to defend the world?" the Oracle asked. That piercing gaze had returned.

"Of course," he added after a brief hesitation. "Of course."

The Oracle sighed, turning away and pacing a few steps. The timid maiden she'd brought along looked back and forth between the two in obvious concern, but if she had something to say, she kept it to herself. The celebration in The Victor's Chalice had resumed, and laughter and music echoed down the street to mingle with the quiet trickling of the fountain by which they'd gathered. They'd have even more to celebrate soon, assuming he wasn't dreaming.

"Glory is not the goal of an Aurora Knight, Prince Darius. Do consider what the Knights stand for before you take this burden on," Ria said softly, breaking the silence. "And I suggest you say farewell to your friends at The Chalice for the night, too. We'll need to make the most of what little time we have. Tomorrow will be busy with preparations, and considering the urgency of things, the day after that you'll be deployed to the Cryptwastes to face what's halted Vatrisland's army. Come, Charise." The young shrine maiden scurried into step behind her superior, and the two began to walk back in the direction of their tower.

"Oracle," Darius called out.

The pair stopped. Charise looked back but Ria continued to face away.

"I'm ready for this. Whatever the problem is, whatever's out there to fight, I'm strong enough to handle it."

"I do not doubt your strength." Then she added, "Goodnight, Prince Vatri."

The Oracle and maiden headed off into the night.

Darius hesitated beside the fountain, weighing his options as he looked back and forth between the castle and The Victor's Chalice. No use trying to sleep just yet, he decided. Besides, his good fortune called for a toast with his friends. What was one more drink before he turned in?

3

Darius cringed at the sunlight streaming in through the north-facing window of his bedroom. His head throbbed. One more drink had turned so quickly into at least five. If he'd had his way, he would have slept until noon, but instead he'd been prodded from bed at his father's command to be cleaned and dressed by hurrying attendants for the special occasion. At least they were nearly finished tugging and buckling the imposing suit of dark crimson and gold full plate armor onto his body. The process always took several minutes, and there was nothing comfortable about the end result. He did, however, look awfully heroic in the full-length mirror before him, clad in a sturdy shell of Vatrisland's colors.

Magnus Vatri, dressed red and decked with gold jewelry looked on, noting with a laugh, "Look at you, boy! You look almost as sharp as I did at your age!"

Darius forced a grin for the dad-and-lad act that his father's cheer called for. "Sure, old man," he offered quietly. Out of the corner of his eye, he could see the attendants glancing at one another and hardening their faces to contain their expressions. He wasn't fooling them.

At last they fastened a red cloak around Darius' neck, bowed, and retreated, their task complete. The prince looked himself over one last time with a satisfied grin.

"Come, son! You look like you need a breath of fresh air. We'll take the balcony instead of the halls." Magnus gestured

Darius to his side. In spite of his hefty, clanking armor and aching hangover, the prince managed to match his father's pace.

The two moved through the corridors of the palace and out onto a long, open-air balcony that overlooked Cloudbreach. Darius stepped up to the railing, taking gulps of cold morning air to sharpen his senses. In spite of the hour and the chill in the air, the city below them hummed with activity of miners, craftsmen, and merchants getting an early start. In his younger days, he'd marveled at all of the tiny people milling around the cobbled streets among the steep roofed houses and shops. They looked like toys from here. Beyond the city walls, sunlit rocky slopes gave way to thickening clusters of evergreen trees and snaking rivers dotted with villages. This southernmost end of Vatrisland brimmed with a rugged terrain that dared men to tame it, and brought out the best in those who met the challenge.

Magnus slid up alongside him. "You know, someday, when I'm gone, this will all be yours. Are you ready to make a name for yourself? Never before has a future king of Vatrisland had such opportunity before him as you will with the power you'll be granted today."

There he went playing dad again. Darius felt more comfortable accepting the act out on the balcony without the attendants listening in. The years spent at odds with his father battled with his desire to take Magnus' new support at face value.

"I'm looking forward to it," Darius said, smiling slightly. "I'd never have dreamed I'd have the chance to wield one of the Aurora Arms though, much less lead the Knights. The Oracle tells me I have you to thank for that."

Magnus laughed quietly. "Well, that old crow talks a good game, but with the proper encouragement, she proved to not be as unyielding as she leads others to believe. Remember that, too. In her position, she'll be giving you a lot of guidance. Don't be afraid to question her if she doesn't seem to have our kingdom's best interests at heart."

Darius nodded. "You've got that right. She was quick to start giving me advice even as she delivered her message last night."

"Oh?" Magnus arched an eyebrow. Suddenly he was all business. "And what did she have to say to you?"

There was no good reason to rile his father up over the Oracle's lecture. Darius shrugged to downplay his comment. "Not much, really. Just seemed to want to remind me of my responsibility to the world. She seemed sincere. I guess she wanted to make sure I had my head on straight before I took on all of this power."

Magnus sighed and massaged his forehead with his fingertips. "Darius, the Oracle preaches from a perspective of traditions over a millennium old. The world is different now. It isn't the overrun wilderness of monsters that it was back then. Today, when men draw lines on maps, those lines mean something. We're organized. We're equipped to defend ourselves now, and our neighbors are too. The world doesn't need the Aurora Knights to come flying to everyone's rescue anymore."

Darius nodded slightly, returning his eyes to the expanse beyond the balcony. "So, if you don't think I need the Titangavel to do what the Oracle's calling the Knights for, what would you have me do?" he asked.

"Do what any man would do in your position with that kind of might. Put all of that muscle and fury of yours to use protecting our interests. The throne will be yours someday, Darius. Use the Aurora Arms and your Knights to ensure that Vatrisland remains the greatest kingdom in all the world for ages to come!"

Darius slumped a bit against the balcony railing. His father's motives were becoming clear, and a tiny mote of disgust took root in his gut. He'd been a fool to think that this opportunity had anything to do with mending the rift between them or appreciating his strengths. He maintained his gaze out over the city, eyes narrowed, sorting his feelings.

Magnus prodded him. "What is it, boy?"

Darius debated for a moment more. He rarely had moments alone with his father, and he might not come back home for some time after this. It would be better to get it off of his chest now. He turned to Magnus, scowling and standing tall. "How long has it been since mother died?"

"Oh, here we go." Exasperation rose in the king's voice.

"Over eleven years now? Eleven years since you last gave half a damn about me and suddenly, out of the blue, we're father and son again when you can make me an Aurora Knight. No more 'big, blond meathead' now that I'm useful, huh?"

"Don't start on this, boy."

But pent up emotions began to bubble to the surface. Darius balled up his fist and struck the railing firmly as he raised his voice. "You made me feel that the thing that made me feel most alive was wasteful and stupid. You tried so many times to make me something else, and now you want to loop my sword arm onto puppet strings and call me 'son'?"

"It was wasteful, boy!" Magnus spat back, startling him. "With the Titangavel in your hands, all of your playing around will finally mean something, but I couldn't have counted on that coming to pass. I had an heir to groom on my own and all you wanted to do was scrap in the dirt. With the Aurora Arms at your command, you can be a warrior king, but without them it's one world or the other. I'm giving you a future you could never have gotten on your own, and you stand here ungrateful because I didn't clap enough for your swordplay?"

"You treated me like I was a burden!"

"So stop your whining and fix it!"

Magnus' words ground the argument to an instant halt. Only the sound of whistling wind sweeping along the balcony passed between them. Darius stared his father down. Now he wished he had never brought the subject up. Beneath his defiant exterior, a chill crept into his gut. He gripped the railing to steady himself.

"You want to hear me speak proudly of you? Want to be my precious son?" Magnus asked gruffly. "Do my will now, and I'll sing your praise from the highest peak above Cloudbreach. I'll beg your forgiveness for never seeing your worth."

Darius replied, but immediately regretted it as he heard his voice crack slightly. "So that's how it'll be then? Go out and fight your way? Earn your pride?"

"If you're going to be like this, I can find another."

It was all that Darius could do to keep from shuddering. "What?"

"Vatrisland is full of others who would gladly fight for me," Magnus continued steadily, as emotionless as if he were talking about a sandwich or tree stump. "She is a kingdom of fighters and patriots. I can think of a dozen in the top ranks of our army alone who would gladly bear my will to every corner of the world at my command, but I offer it to you first. Now will you do this for me, or should I find someone more suitable?"

Darius looked out again across the expanse beyond the balcony. What a twisted ultimatum. He gritted his teeth hard enough that he worried they'd crack.

"The morning is escaping us."

"I'll do it." Darius managed to pry his jaws apart. "I'll fight for us first."

"Swear it."

"What?"

Magnus was still an emotionless stone wall. "I know you, son. Your mother raised you to honor your word. Your oath is your bond, so swear now that you'll serve me and Vatrisland without question."

31

Darius knelt woodenly before Magnus and looked up, wondering how he had now found an even greater shame than agreeing to earn his father's pride. From the lower vantage point, he felt like a child now in every way. "I swear that I will serve you without question."

"For the glory of Vatrisland?"

"For the glory," Darius whispered.

"Good. Rise," the king commanded. Darius stood.

"I will go on ahead to Aurora Tower," Magnus said, turning away. "Wait here until you've composed yourself. Don't show up looking all sullen and embarrass me." He crossed the rest of the balcony and vanished into the castle.

Darius remained there on the balcony letting the wind whip over him. His frustration churned within him until it boiled over in an angry roar into the morning sky. He made a fist once more and punched the cold stone wall of the castle.

Flexing the pain out of his knuckles, he walked swiftly through the halls and out toward Aurora Tower.

XXX

Darius shielded his eyes as he approached the shining tower that housed the Aurora Arms. It stood out against the stark stone walls of that castle masonry around it as a spire of white and gold, gradually narrowing as it reached higher and higher into the sky. Glowing tracery worked into its artful design pulsed periodically, making clear to anyone who might try to breach its walls that they'd have to dispel dangerous magical wards first. Further protection from the mighty walls of his family's ancestral castle made Aurora Tower a fortress within a fortress, well protected from monsters and thieves.

The tower's great double doors stood wide open today, and two shrine maidens attending the doorway bowed to Darius as he

32

entered. They dipped further and more reverently than usual, he noticed. No doubt they'd already been made aware of his new role. He nodded slightly to each one as he passed them and walked through the entrance hall toward the lift platform at the back of the building. The marble interior and towering statues of past heroes glowed with heroic glory under shafts of sunlight streaming in. White banners with the Knights' crest in gold swayed in a gentle breeze that snaked into the chamber through windows set high on the walls.

As Darius approached the lift, he spotted the Oracle and his father waiting there for him side-by-side. Both smiled at his arrival, and the prince forced his own out in return. He suspected it was as much an effort for them as it was for him.

The Oracle bowed slightly. "Welcome, Prince Vatri."

"Are you ready, boy?" Magnus asked. His practiced, carefree grin gave no clue of their argument minutes earlier. Darius wished he could cast aside his own feelings as easily.

"I'm ready, yeah." Darius didn't make eye contact with either as Ria commanded the broad, golden platform bearing the three to ascend the floors of the tower.

Quiet song echoed down the shaft as the three were carried upward, growing louder and more distinct as they went. The high, sweet voices of shrine maidens harmonized in a glorious anthem that Darius had never heard before.

In greatest need, and darkest hour,
we'll endure each foe and fright.
For to succeed, 'gainst evil's power,
we shall serve our Aurora Knights.

"You do well to pay attention, Darius." The Oracle's smile grew more genuine as she saw him craning and listening. "They're reaffirming their loyalty to the bearers of the Aurora Arms. Once you are charged with your weapon, all the resources of the Tower and the maidens housed here will be sworn to your command."

"That's all it takes?" the king murmured under his breath, also looking upward.

Darius ignored his father. "But isn't the point of the Aurora Arms' powers, that the Knights can handle whatever arises on their own?"

Ria shook her head. "You will be powerful beyond your imagining, for certain, but not every evil can be slain with power alone. The shrine maidens will support you from here to make you and your knights even more capable. They're well versed in ancient lore, trained to act as diplomatic liaisons with cultures around the world, and some are even capable of magic and combat should times get so desperate. With their expertise at your disposal, you and your Knights won't just be mighty in battle, you'll be truly unstoppable."

Darius nodded, taking in more of the song. The maidens sang their oath to face any challenge in service to their Knights. They vowed to pick themselves back up no matter how despair crushed their spirits. Few legends of the Aurora Knights that he'd heard had ever mentioned the maidens, and even then, only briefly, but just as an army needed logistical support, so did the Knights. He'd never known how much happened behind the scenes to ensure victory over the great terrors of the past.

The platform that lifted them came to a stop at the top floor, and the singing shrine maidens burst into a loud chorus right on cue. Several dozen of the red and white robed servants crowded the chamber, forced close together by the tables and chairs that had been pushed snug to the walls, leaving only a narrow path that the three walked toward the floating Aurora Crystal at the center of the room.

The king and the Oracle took up positions on either side of the man-sized gem, leaving the prince standing before it, facing sealed double doors the full length of the far wall that hadn't been cast open in nearly a century. Darius' feelings of anger and resentment toward his father began to melt away in the presence of the Aurora Crystal, as though it willed him to set aside lesser concerns in favor of a nobler calling.

The singing maidens quieted their song to a gentle hum as the Oracle spoke. "As Oracle of the Arms and bearer of the Inner Key, I have sworn to only deploy the Aurora Arms in times of great need, and only for the defense of mankind. It is my belief that the time of need draws near. In response to the gathering undead army to the north, and the unprecedented show of power from the necromancer at its command, I deem the assembly of a team of Aurora Knights to be a necessary precaution. May our Knights defend us until peace is secured, and the Arms are committed to the vault once again."

She turned to Magnus and addressed him. "King Magnus Vatri, as King of Vatrisland and bearer of the Outer Key, do you concur that the threats I have described demand the deployment of the Arms, and the assembly of a team of Aurora Knights?"

Darius spotted Magnus' subtle smile. Clearly his father was enjoying this public opportunity to demonstrate his role as a check to the Oracle's power. The king hesitated just long enough for some in the room to take notice before he answered her. "I concur."

Ria nodded at King Magnus, then each reached beneath their collars and pulled out a finger-length crystalline shard, the king's on an ornate chain, and the Oracle's on a braided leather loop. Each crystal emitted a soft glow as its owner gripped it. The maidens' song surged back to its full volume as the two leaders reached out toward the Aurora Crystal, found the small divots in its surface that each fit their respective shards, and set them in place with a quiet clink.

The prismatic light emanating from the center of the

Aurora Crystal flared brighter, and a rising hum filled the room, challenging the shrine maidens to reach a triumphant crescendo to be heard over it. The crystal descended slowly into a golden frame in the floor like a key into a lock, and settled into its final position with a quiet click. At once, motes of light began to crawl from the lock along lines in the floor, much like the lights that traced the tower's exterior walls.

Darius had seen many impressive and exotic things in his days as prince, but now he watched in awe as the lights made their way to the massive pair of doors at the far end of the room and crawled their way to the Knights' crest that joined the two sides together. The crest lit up as brightly as the mystical aurora shined in the night sky, and the doors slowly slid apart, producing a passage so wide that it joined the outer shrine and inner vault as a single larger space.

The shrine maidens concluded their song, and even began to break disciplined form, some quietly congratulating one another on keeping the hymn going through the whole process, others peering into the now open vault. Darius stepped past the Aurora Crystal, now nested in the socket on the ground, and looked to the Oracle. Whatever doubts she might have had about him, she didn't show. She offered a slight smile and gestured to him to cross the threshold with her. The prince smiled back and strode forward proudly, his shoulders pulled back, like he'd been taught to do during public appearances.

Magelamps set into the walls slowly lit to their full illumination as Darius entered. The vault was equipped as an elaborate war room. A pair of circular mirrors, similar to one his father owned, hung at opposite ends of the room. Assuming they bore the same enchantments, they could be used to communicate across the world to anyone else with a similar mirror. Many rulers and particularly rich merchants had them.

At the center of the vault sat a large round stone table, at least six feet in length. In the middle of it, a circle of glowing runes emitted a top-down view of Aurora Tower and the surrounding landscape. He immediately recognized the layout of Cloudbreach and the highest mountain peaks that ran along Vatrisland's southernmost, sea-facing border. The glowing illusory map looked perfectly accurate.

And then he saw them on the far wall.

The Aurora Arms.

A shaft of light shined down upon each one, clasped in the hands of a statue of its original bearer. He approached them, recognizing them all instantly.

Faegrip, Staff of Guile. A shaft of shimmering silver topped with a midnight purple amethyst.

Freestar, Hope's Sabre. A curved sword with a hand guard bearing a sapphire of vivid blue.

Highbeacon, Herald of Brilliance. A slender spear with a head of fiery yellow topaz.

Watchward, the Vigilant. A bow of intricately carved pale wood with a vibrant emerald mounted on its grip.

And Titangavel, the Maul of Justice. A shining hammer nearly as long as the prince was tall. A steel and gold symbol of leadership decked with a blood red ruby in the middle of its head. None of the artists who had depicted it had done the glorious weapon justice, and Darius' heartbeat quickened in its presence.

The Oracle stepped into his view, breaking his fascination. "Prince Darius Vatri, today you take up the mantle of the Aurora Knight. Vile forces will be tireless in their efforts to drive our world to despair with furious wrath and cunning manipulation. You are charged to assemble a team of talented, trustworthy comrades, on whom you will bestow the remaining four Aurora Arms. Together, you will be the most powerful line of defense that mankind has ever brought to bear, and you will pursue those who sow terror and destruction until the world can rest easy once more."

The prince nodded. "Yes, Oracle."

"And do you vow to uphold the traditions and values of the Aurora Knights? To put the safety of the world first above else, and to command each Knight you recruit to do likewise? To fight the forces of evil and destruction that only you and yours can stop?"

Darius froze. Time seemed to slow to a crawl. The Oracle's infamous piercing gaze bored into him. There was no way she could know what he had discussed with his father in the past hour, could she? He hazarded a glance at Magnus out of the corner of his eye, but could only barely see his face at the current angle.

The king winked.

Or did he? Darius could only see one side of his father's face. Beads of sweat gathered beneath the prince's stifling heavy armor. He wracked his brain for a way to make and keep two oaths at odds with one another. If he refused now he could at least preserve his honor, but he would never have another chance to lead the Knights.

His mouth dried, but he managed to force his words out loudly and clearly. "I swear."

His father didn't react. Maybe he just assumed his son was making the oath as a formality; that Darius' true loyalty stayed with Vatrisland first.

If the Oracle could sense his nervousness, she didn't show it. She smiled as she continued, "Then take up the Titangavel. I bestow upon you the title of Knight-Captain of the Aurora Knights." She stepped aside, leaving nothing between him and the open arms of the statue that bore his weapon.

Darius stepped forward and reached up, grasping the long haft of the Titangavel with both hands. A tingling rush ripped through his system, and he let out an uncontrolled gasp. The hammer glowed with radiance as he held it. All of the symptoms of his hangover cleared. The throbbing in his knuckles from punching solid stone earlier dulled first, then faded away completely. Even the burden of his armor felt as light as ordinary clothing. He looked the hammer up and down in awe. It was as though he'd never truly been alive until this moment. Pure vitality coursed through his veins.

"Prince Darius Vatri," the Oracle declared, "as the Oracle of the Arms, I hereby bind to you Titangavel, the Maul of Justice. Until you restore it to this sanctum, it will recognize no other master with its powers. Take up this weapon and defend the world in the face of its most desperate hour. As of this day, you are Knight-Captain of the Aurora Knights."

The shrine maidens broke into thunderous applause with happy smiles on their faces at the Oracle's triumphant conclusion. So too did his father. Darius thrust the hammer high in the air one-handed, and they roared for him all the louder. For that moment, all of his worries about honor and oaths, family and duty—all of it faded away.

4

After the ceremony ended, many of the shrine maidens scattered throughout the room and began pulling books from the nearby shelves, spreading them across the tables, and taking notes. Darius managed to cast a glance over some of the open tomes. They were filled with images of monsters, relics, and historical figures.

Other maidens set to contacting important emissaries from all over the continent using the magic mirrors. Darius recognized the faces of many figures he'd seen visit the castle before. Their reactions were mixed. Some took the news that the Aurora Knights were being assembled seriously. Others refused to believe that anything so bad could be going on that it called for action. Whatever responses the shrine maidens faced though, they spoke with composed calm, several even in the native language of their contact.

A firm slap on his shoulder jarred Darius from his observations. "Come, son!" Magnus boomed. "Let's not let that hammer go to waste. We need to show you off to the people!"

"King Magnus," the Oracle cut in, "with respect, we don't have time for that. Darius needs to train with his new powers this afternoon so that he can be headed toward the Cryptwastes by tomorrow morning."

The king scoffed. "Don't be silly, Oracle. Darius may be your Knight-Captain now, but he's also the Prince of Vatrisland. His people need to see him in all of his glory. Isn't that right, boy?"

The two looked at him expectantly. The weight of his two promises crashed back onto his shoulders.

He couldn't turn away a chance to parade the streets like the heroes of Vatrisland did when they returned from battle. This was what he'd always wanted. "I'm a fast learner, Oracle," he promised her. "I'll be fine. We'll get at it later tonight."

"See? That's the way!" Magnus cheered.

Ria pressed her mouth into a slight frown. "Very well, Darius," she huffed. She turned and went back to work with her maidens.

The prince joined his father and the two strode briskly through the castle and out the front gate. A two-tiered chariot pulled by a pair of hulking riding hounds awaited Darius, along with a dozen trumpeters and the unit of soldiers that he'd been a part of until last night. He searched the ranks and chuckled to himself. Bainon and Ottrick stood beside one another in formation, craning their necks to smirk at him and nudging one another subtly with their elbows.

Darius shook his head and hopped easily onto the upper platform of the chariot. "Get on your way, then," Magnus commanded the driver. "And take your time. I want everyone to get a chance to see him."

The chariot rocked forward. Ahead of Darius, the trumpets sounded Vatrisland's anthem, and the steady footfalls of the soldiers joined in, adding percussion. The group descended into the city, toward the cheering crowds.

XXX

The parade had excited Darius, but his thrill at being trotted around like a show dog faded when his father dragged him to a reception at the castle. After a few hours spent making small talk with courtiers, he nearly bounded out the door when a rather bubbly shrine maiden came to ask if he'd still be training that night.

"Oh, come Prince Vatri. You're stepping out before I finish my story?" cooed a clingy countess.

"Duty calls, I'm afraid." he apologized hastily, already halfway to the exit. "You'll have to catch me with it another time!"

The prince and the shrine maiden squeezed through the last crowd of nobles and out into the hallway. "I think you may have saved my life just now," he confided in the girl once they were safely out of earshot, eliciting a cheerful laugh.

In a few short minutes the two reached the army's drill yard. Darius strode out onto the open expanse still fully armored, hefting the Titangavel over his shoulder one-handed. The Oracle awaited him there, along with her timid aide and around twenty shrine maidens, all armed with enchanted focusing staffs to aid spellcasting. The troops had been called into a nearby mess hall for dinner, so they had the whole yard to themselves. The prince grinned. If the tales of the Knights' powers did the real thing any justice, he'd need all the space he could get.

Ria arched an eyebrow at Darius, smirking slightly. "You look eager, Darius. I trust a few hours spent chattering with the monarchy have left you keen to express yourself?"

Darius gave his weapon a few tentative twirls. "Not gonna lie; I'm ready to break something."

"Let's see what you're made of, then. The maidens I've brought with me here are well-versed in summoning beasts. Are you ready to test your prowess?"

Darius nodded, bringing the Titangavel to the ready. The Oracle motioned forward five shrine maidens, who rushed to her side and struck a combat-ready stance with steely focus in their eyes. They held their focusing staffs out before them awaiting her next command.

Ria gave her order. "Whipwolves."

The maidens concentrated, gathering wisps of glowing power around the hoop-shaped heads of their staffs. When they'd gathered enough power, the wisps leapt forward and coalesced into snarling forms. The wolves quickly moved to surround Darius, bounding easily about the open field. Lean muscles rippled visibly under their sleek, gray coats. They wriggled their long, barbed tails back and forth over their heads like scorpions and snapped at him with hunger in their eyes. Only the viscous golden fog running down their bodies and legs hinted that they were constructs of magic and not genuine wild creatures.

Darius had never fought whipwolves before, but had heard tales from the soldiers who had lost friends to them. They brought down prey by dashing past and catching their barbs on loose fabric or flesh. An ordinary man yanked to the ground rarely had time to find his feet before the rest of the pack pounced on top of him.

He smirked confidently. He was far from ordinary now. He shifted the Titangavel from one hand into both and spun back and forth nimbly to keep them all in sight. His pulse quickened as he waited for an opening.

The first one darted toward him. It came in low across his shins, but he swung the weapon across, burying the hammer's head into its face. What would have been a gory display against a real predator in the wilderness only resulted in a burst of magical mist here as the summoned wolf dispersed.

He twisted to see a trio rushing in from behind to capitalize on him being out of position after his last swing, but he moved nimbly in spite of his heavy armor. With lightning speed, he shifted the Titangavel back into one hand and used his free hand to catch a leaping wolf by the throat and slam it down upon the next one, plowing his hand all the way through them and cracking the packed dirt as the two disintegrated. The third wolf sped past him, catching its tail barb where two plates of his armor met, but with his new might, Darius simply dug his heel into the ground. The predator yelped in surprise as its tail pulled taut, bringing it to an instant, painful stop. A hammering overhead blow finished the job, rumbling the drill yard as it landed.

Out of the corner of his eye, Darius noticed a soldier leaving the mess hall. The man spotted the action, doubled back, and returned followed by an audience, which quickly poured out of the building. He split a broad smile and laughed, thrilled to have a crowd as the last wolf pounced on his back. It plunged its jaws toward his neck, only to get a mouthful of gauntlet-clad fist as he brought an arm back to block the bite. With a twist of his wrist, he grasped its upper teeth like a handle and yanked the creature over his head, slamming it into the ground on its back.

Everyone cheered and hooted, except for the Oracle and her maidens. Darius was still close enough to see her stern glare in the setting sun as she called more maidens forward. The women gathered into three trios at her next command.

"Jinra."

"Bring it on! Wait, wha—?" Darius' thrill stopped short as he processed what he had just heard.

Each trio tapped the hooped heads of their staffs together, gathering their powers. In a blinding flash, a three-story tall muscular humanoid with long, curved horns, blood-red skin, and fists wreathed in crackling fire sprung from each group of summoners. The crowd of onlookers backpedaled as the giants glowered down at Darius, bearing mouths full of savage fangs. Darius laughed nervously. Would it have killed her to give him a step between this one and the last one?

He shook off his uncertainties and bounded into action, dodging a searing punch that crashed to the ground just beside him. He bolted at the nearest jinra and laid into its shin with a sideways swing of the Titangavel. The impact echoed wet and loud like a butcher's work tenderizing meat, but the towering figure barely budged, then retaliated, batting him away with an open-handed swat. Darius skidded backward, grunting as fire scorched his skin. It was everything he could do to dig his weapon into the ground, slowing himself to a stop about a dozen yards away. He panted and struggled through pain-blurred vision to keep his eyes on the massive shapes stomping toward him.

The Oracle's voice cut through the chaos. She sounded close. Hadn't she been at the other end of the drill yard? "Is that all you've got? I can call them off if you're tired," she goaded him.

She was taunting him now? Cute. Darius stood tall and scoffed. "Please. Are these the scariest things your maidens could come up with? I'm just warming up," he fired back.

But as the giants closed in, he wracked his brain for a new approach. He'd already felt himself moving faster and hitting harder than he'd ever dreamed possible, but it just wasn't enough. If he was going to win this fight, he needed to find the scope of his new powers.

He needed to get higher.

Darius bolted forward, slipping between the legs of one of the jinra as they stomped at him. He cleared their shadows and looked up, spotting a warehouse that looked just a touch taller than his foes. That would do it, if the legends of the Aurora Knights' powers hadn't exaggerated.

He coiled his legs down and pushed off with all of his might. His muscles, infused with the power of the Titangavel, launched him high into the air. He rocketed over the heads of the soldiers, then higher above the roof of the mess hall and onward, cresting the lip of the warehouse roof and landing as nimbly as a house cat.

Darius gasped, trying to calm his racing heart. He looked out over not just the drill yard, but even farther down to the city and the woods beyond it as he struggled to wrap his mind around fighting on this empowering new scale. Just below him, the crowd roared even louder, but the jinra were less impressed. They turned and continued their tireless pursuit, refusing to give him time to appreciate the power in his hands.

He faced the jinra once more, looking them straight in the eyes as his mouth spread into a cocky smile. With a furious roar and a running start, he launched himself across the expanse, hurtling like a cannonball toward the nearest one's head with the Titangavel wound back. The giant reached to swat Darius from the sky, but the prince shot past the hand, driving his weapon headfirst into its eye.

The jinra howled in pain, clawing at its face to smash him, but Darius was already gone. Having swung atop its head, he braced himself for balance with a hand on one of its tree trunk-like horns. He turned his gaze back and forth quickly, struggling to keep all of his foes in sight. A second jinra swung a pair of clenched fists down to smash him, but the lumbering giant couldn't match his speed. He leapt from his perch to the ground, landing in a clean forward roll and springing to his feet. The blow crushed the monster's head, collapsing it in a burst of mist.

Two to go.

The remaining pair of jinra bounded toward him, hunching low and spreading their arms wide to block him from escaping the corner of the drill yard. Darting beneath them wouldn't work this time.

The answer came to his mind in a flash of inspiration. Legends detailed Titangavel's power over earth and stone. All he had to do was figure out exactly how to use them.

The moment he wondered how to make the powers work, instincts began to creep into his head. He envisioned great jagged rocks bursting up from the ground to trip his enemies. With all his willpower, he concentrated on the ground before the oncoming monsters and swung the Titangavel in a rising arc across the front of his body like a conductor guiding an orchestra.

The ground lurched in front of him, projecting thick spikes of solid stone. Some gouged one of the jinra in its shins. Others caught its foot, tripping it and sending it plummeting toward the ground. Darius bounded a few yards back in a single leap and swung the weapon again, this time straight up. More spikes burst upward, in a neat line. The jinra failed to keep itself from landing on them throat first.

One left.

The Oracle spoke. This time her voice sounded far away again. "Whipwolves."

Another pack of predators sprung from the heads of the maidens' staffs. Darius struggled to divide his attention between the last approaching jinra and the new targets. Even with the power of the Titangavel running through him, exhaustion began to burn in his muscles. He needed more room to maneuver than he had, or things were going to get ugly fast.

The giant sneered and lifted a massive leg to stomp down on the prince. A scorching gust of air raced across him as he dodged out from beneath the falling foot. The whipwolves were right there waiting for him, though, denying him a chance to leap clear of the melee.

Desperate to be out from under the jinra's shadow, he hopped onto its foot and began to race up its outstretched leg at a full run. Only a little higher, and he could bound out of the chaos and get his bearings.

Then they struck. Hundreds of pounds of fur and fangs collided with him halfway up the muscular red shin. His limbs tangled with the pair of leaping whipwolves and the three went spiraling back onto the dirt. Four more were on him in an instant. He struggled to bat them off while still covering his exposed face with armored arms, but they were in closer than the Titangavel's reach. A burning fist from above slammed down on his legs and pelvis, burning and crushing him along with some of the wolves.

Wild, blinding pain ripped through his body, forcing an agonized cry from his lungs.

Terror gripped Darius. He flailed in panic. He couldn't feel his legs. Why couldn't he feel his legs? The fist pulled up off of them, lifting into the sky like a blazing summer sun, slowing, then coming back down straight toward his head. He squeezed his eyes shut and cried out again.

"Enough!"

At the ringing voice of the Oracle, the brightening flare beyond his eyelids faded. The rasping and snapping quieted and the weight lifted from his arms and chest. His eyes squinted open, but refused to see properly, producing only a messy mix of evening sky and indistinct lights. Agonizing pain punctuated every breath he took, but he forced himself to continue. In, then out.

Don't stop. Again. In, then out.

Through the haze of pain, a single set of footsteps tapped toward him. The Oracle spoke quietly, now near him, "Just wait. Don't struggle."

He couldn't obey. Little fearful whimpers escaped his trembling mouth as he strained to move his legs. Still, no feeling.

"Wait," she said again forcefully.

Though he battled his will to do it, this time Darius obeyed. Tingling warmth spread through his body, slowly but surely. Feeling crept back down his abdomen, down his legs, then to his feet. Trickling sensations running down his skin and blistering burns dulled, then ceased. In the longest minute of his life, his body had knit itself back together from the brink.

His jaw stopped shaking. Now he took in more regular breaths between panting. He rolled to onto his hands and knees, his crooked, battered armor groaning as he pried himself free of the impact crater left by the jinra's blow. The soldiers looking on started to silently disperse. The shrine maidens that had summoned the monsters now gathered close to one another whispering and pointing, looking worried. He'd been reduced to a bloodied heap before their eyes. Darius flushed and fumed, pulling himself to his feet, and fixed an angry glare on the Oracle. "So you brought me out here to kick me around in front of everyone, huh? Show me who's boss for blowing you off earlier? That it?" he accused her.

The Oracle narrowed her eyes at him, "Do you really think me that petty?" she countered quietly.

He grew louder. "Then why beat me within an inch of my life? You almost crippled your own Knight-Captain. Do you want me to face down the darkness from a chair, cause it would be damned hard to fight without legs!"

"Don't be so dramatic." She maintained her unaffected calm. "I asked nothing of you that you couldn't survive with the power of the Titangavel running through you. You're already back on your feet, and by the time you go to sleep tonight, you won't have a scratch left on you."

Easy for her to say. She hadn't had to wonder if she'd ever walk again. The faces of the soldiers and shrine maidens kept running through his mind. He couldn't imagine what must they have thought about the future of the Aurora Knights, watching him be thrown around like a rag doll.

"Do you know what you did wrong? Why you were beaten?" she continued.

Now she was going to lecture him in front of all of them? Maybe his father was right to not trust this old crow. This was her first time actually commanding the Aurora Knights. She had romanticized them to the point that they had to be unstoppable, and now she was ready to blame him when these powers weren't all she had imagined.

"Nothing," Darius said defiantly. "You know what? Not a thing! I was completely outmatched! Nobody could have handled that, even with the Titangavel!"

"Exactly."

Darius cocked his head, speechless.

"You're completely new at this, just growing accustomed to your powers," the Oracle explained, pacing slowly as she spoke. "This isn't drill yard dueling or stag hunting. This is your first taste of the chaos of real battle, and all of the fury in the world won't save you when vicious undead descend upon you from all sides. It will be unfair. You'll be outnumbered, surprised, and pursued whether you're ready or not."

He looked away from her. He didn't want to let go of his anger, but as much as he hated to admit it, she had a point. He had great prowess and natural talent, but what real, raw combat had he experienced? At the height of this battle, he'd been reduced to whimpering terror when the monsters had overcome him.

The Oracle softened her judgmental tone. "It is up to you to select four more Knights to aid you. At the very least, I suggest you choose your second-in-command before you begin fighting in earnest. Someone who knows war well, and can watch your back. Someone whose command men don't question to back you up and support your decisions. A number of your father's seasoned generals are already deployed to the Cryptwastes. Perhaps one of them would be suitable for the task."

Darius nodded. Though he rarely struggled to get others to like him, no amount of good intention could make up for his lack of command experience. Not only would one of his father's generals fill that blind spot, he'd also be another Knight loyal to Vatrisland. Finally, an easy decision. Something that would please his father and already had the Oracle's blessing.

"Okay," Darius confirmed. "I'm on board, but there's just one problem. How do I choose the right man for the job? I've talked to some of them in passing at parties and such, but not enough to make the call. I can't just hand one of these over to anyone." He gestured to the Titangavel as he finished.

At this, the Oracle waved over some of the shrine maidens

who had summoned the monsters that tested him. Charise scampered over quickly, but the others took a little more time, still staggered from the exhausting task of maintaining massive jinra that had ground him into the dirt. At first, they didn't make eye contact with him.

Darius cleared his throat. "Hey, no hard feelings, okay? You really pushed me to fight harder back there. I needed it."

The women relaxed a bit and nodded. "Yes, Prince Darius," they agreed.

The Oracle went on. "Recall that all of the maidens serving at the tower are at your disposal. Ask them to help you with what you need. You'll find them quicker and smarter than much of the castle staff, I assure you."

He looked on them again and they straightened and saluted. "Okay, then. I guess I need whatever records you can bring me for all of the generals serving out in the Cryptwastes right now. Just tell the castle's archivist that you're pulling the military records with my permission, and take anything useful you find up to my quarters."

Except for Charise, who remained with the Oracle, the shrine maidens nodded at him again and hustled off toward the castle. It was encouraging to see them snap into action with such zeal. Darius was used to being waited upon, but he could detect a wholeheartedness from these women that the castle staff lacked.

"Well," the Oracle said, straightening her robes as she spoke, "with that settled, you may want to address one last thing before you clean yourself up." She glanced toward the drill yard.

Darius looked back over the formerly level field and managed an impressed chuckle. The whole yard was torn and gouged to pieces from his fight. Massive spikes of earth he'd conjured up still remained, some standing as he'd left them, others split and toppled over. Long divots from where he'd skidded across the ground wove between the fist and footprints that the jinra had left behind from their strikes. In mere minutes, he and the beasts had rendered the landscape a blasted mess.

The sight thoroughly satisfied him.

He extended the Titangavel out before him at arm's length and waved it in a single, level arc. The expanse churned like fluid for a moment, settled, became solid again. The soldiers would find it more even than it had been before his arrival when they drilled tomorrow.

The Oracle cracked an agreeable smile. "Is this the first time this prince has straightened up after his own party?"

Darius shrugged, grinning casually. "Wouldn't have been very knightly of me to leave a mess behind. I've got a tradition to uphold now. I've got to be civil and thoughtful."

She rolled her eyes and headed toward Aurora Tower, beckoning her shy aide to follow. "Well I hope you won't hold it against me if I'm still skeptical. Get your rest once you've gone over those records. I'll see you off to the Cryptwastes tomorrow morning."

"Right, will do." Darius turned to walk toward the castle, but stopped short as his previously pristine armor ground awkwardly against itself. He ran his fingers over the cracks and dents that locked the plates together at several joints, shaking his head and laughing softly. Good thing he had asked the castle's master smith to craft two suits when he'd had it commissioned. He made a mental note to order a third as he lopsidedly hobbled inside.

XXX

Darius struggled to convince himself that there was any merit in leaving the magically warmed stone tub set into the floor of his bathing chamber, where he had soaked nearly all of the day's soreness out of his exhausted muscles. He splayed his arms wide and let neck go slack against the rim, unconsciously drumming the fingers of his right hand on the handle of the Titangavel. Though the Oracle had said that the weapon and its powers were bound to him, leaving it out of sight just felt wrong, and it lay on the floor beside the tub, reassuringly close.

The Oracle. Maybe she wasn't so bad after all. It seemed like they were beginning to reach an understanding, and her advice to him had ultimately been sound. Maybe he could somehow get her to come to a middle ground of some kind with his father about his duties. Surely she'd understand if he kept a slightly closer eye on his own home than he did on the rest of the world. Nobody was completely without favoritism. To expect otherwise of a man was just unrealistic.

He pulled his head up from the tub's rim to look himself over. True to the Oracle's word, his body showed no evidence of the trauma it had endured only hours earlier. If anything, he only looked stronger, his muscles even more defined than before. Little aches were his only reminder that he'd been thrashed earlier, and if her implication that it took time for him to fully master his new powers was accurate, he suspected that someday he might not even suffer this weariness. It was an appealing thought considering that he looked forward to his next fight, hungry for greater glory.

Satisfied that he was intact, the prince stepped out of the tub and began to towel himself off. A knock sounded from the door of his bedroom out beyond the bath chamber. Perhaps that was one of the Oracle's maidens with the records he needed. He quickly tied the towel at his waist, strode over, and tugged the door open.

"I've got those records you—" The Oracle's assistant trailed off into a mess of vowel sounds upon coming face-to-face with the prince's bare chest, her cheeks flushing as red as her robes. The stack of records teetered back and forth in her hands, dropping two scrolls to the floor.

Darius grinned, enjoying seeing the girl disarmed. "Whoa, lost a couple there. Let me." He squatted down and gathered the dropped scrolls, adding, "Go ahead and set your stack down on the writing desk over there."

"O-okay!" the girl stammered her high-pitched reply. She rushed past him to the window-facing desk at the far side of the room and set the documents down. She continued facing the window after she did so, running her fingers along the edges and corners of the stack over and over until it was uniformly box-like on all sides.

The prince tossed the scrolls he'd gathered onto his bed. "I think you've got 'em. They probably can't get much straighter than that, so unless there's anything else...." He trailed off, expecting her to scurry out.

Instead she worked up to speaking again, still facing the window. "I—erm. Rather, I mean...The Oracle...She told me to ask if y-you wanted any help. Going through it. Them! The records, that is."

Darius thought for a minute, torn between having mercy on the poor shy thing and keeping her around. He was certainly tired, and would get things done sooner with help. Military records were unlikely anywhere near as interesting as the bards' songs their actions inspired, and he'd never been much of a reader.

"That would help, yeah," he answered. "Go ahead and have a seat at the desk."

Her body went rigid for a moment, but she managed to loosen up and seat herself. "Yes Prince Vatri."

She hesitated before reaching for the papers. Darius stepped closer with his hands on his hips and prompted her, "So, who are the most promising candidates then?"

"Right!" The girl snapped into action. "Well, I took a look through what the other girls found and I think there's actually only one general who meets all your needs."

"Now hold on. What are my needs?"

"Sorry!" She spun away from the documents to address him to his face before seeming to remember why she'd been so intent on looking away in the first place. Seeing him in only his towel again, she snapped back into position and pushed her glasses up evenly on her nose. "O-okay! So we need someone who's both young enough, you know, to fight and such. But also someone who's b-been recognized for being able to lead men in battle too. And, also, it would be even better if that were someone who was deployed out in the Cryptwastes right now, you know, since that's where you're headed."

Darius nodded. "Makes sense. Okay, go on." He stepped back from the girl, intending to dress himself so that this process didn't take half the night. As cute as this display was, he had to give her a break. He opened a wardrobe on the other side of the room and rooted around for sleepwear.

"So like I said, you've got a great general. General Maxos Riggs. He's twenty-eight, so he's young enough. He has numerous medals for leadership on the battlefield and he's recognized as an extremely capable fighter."

Darius found the clothes he'd been looking for and began to dress. "Mm. And he's dispatched out to the Cryptwastes as we speak?"

"Mm-hmm. He's been out there since autumn and..." She trailed off.

"And?" he asked. He turned his head to one side. Out of the corner of his eye he saw her whip back to facing the window, banging her knee on the desk.

The girl chirped through clenched teeth, "He's great! A perfect match, really!"

The prince shook his head, finished slipping into a silk shirt and pants, and walked back over to the desk. The girl didn't rub her bumped knee, but scrunched and puckered her lips, squinting as she did. He looked past her at the general's credentials. He did indeed seem like a great match. "Well, if it's all the same, I think I'll give him a little interview out there and make my decision in-person. I can do that, right?"

The maiden nodded. She looked at him and half-smiled with her lips pressed tight. She seemed a bit less anxious now that he was fully dressed.

"Good, good. It was nice to have it narrowed down like that. Go ahead and leave this stuff here in case I need another look."

She nodded once more and pushed out from the desk, scraping the chair noisily along the floor as she did. Darius stopped her one last time before she got out the door, "I've seen you tagging along with the Oracle a lot, but I didn't quite catch your name. Sherri, or something?"

The mousey girl faced him one last time. A single limp lock of dull brown hair poked down from under her cap and hung in front of her glasses, "I-it was Charise. And yes, Miss Ria is having me assist her, so you'll probably see me a lot."

He grinned at her. "Thanks, Charise. You've been really helpful."

The girl blushed. Her green eyes lit up. For the first time since she'd arrived at his chamber, Charise returned him a full, if nervous, smile. She turned and closed the door behind her. Darius flopped into his bed for the last night he'd sleep in his own room for some time.

5

As she stood searching the bookshelves at the top chamber of Aurora Tower, Ria startled herself the handful of shrine maidens assigned to night duty when she let out a sudden, relieved laugh. The maidens looked up from their books and stations, wondering what could possibly be funny in tomes of ancient legends and lore, but The Oracle just shook her head. "Sorry. I'm just happy things are finally moving in the right direction."

The women smiled back at her and returned to their work. Stacks of works with any reference to the Cryptwastes and civilizations that had inhabited the area throughout history had already been set aside to be scoured for any hint of what might be worth hiding out among the ruins. Beside those, another stack of books about necromancy and dark powers awaited research. The maidens would index and cross reference every scrap of information Darius sent back to them to narrow their search, but until more information came, they strove to learn as much as they could.

Ria sought to turn her attention back to the shelves, but a blonde maiden approached, coming from within the vault. "Oracle, I've finished contacting the rulers of the surrounding nations, as well as their top advisers and scholars. They all know what we're working with now, and promised they'd contact us if they discovered anything relevant to the effort. What would you like me to do next?"

The Oracle smiled warmly. Since the moment she'd woken

from her sleep, so many of her shrine maidens had been volunteering to work double duty. She almost feared they'd burn themselves out in their zeal. "You've already stayed late to get everything done. Go get some sleep. I want you to be fresh for whatever tomorrow brings."

The woman seemed to debate denying her tiredness for a moment, but a sudden yawn gave her away. She rubbed her eyelids with her fingers and bid Ria goodnight. As she left the chamber, she nearly bumped into another maiden on her way into the room.

Charise had returned. She timidly apologized to the tired woman on her way in and approached Ria, who immediately slipped the books she'd been sorting through back onto the shelf, and looked upon her young maiden hopefully.

"How did it go? What did he say?" the Oracle asked, just above a whisper.

Charise's cheeks were flushed. The girl refused to make eye contact as she began, "W-well, I think he just wanted to get it over with. He said he'd look over the records, and that he'd interview General Riggs, but I think he's just happy that he doesn't have a bunch of options to sort through."

Ria sighed with relief. The subtle flutter that had been gnawing at her stomach since she'd sent Charise to see the prince subsided. If Darius was as eager as Charise made him sound to have his second-in-command chosen, she could likely rest easy.

"It sounds like things went well, then. Why are you still so nervous?"

"Well, he was kind of, a little," Charise paused, searching for the right word, "n-natural."

Ria raised an eyebrow. "How natural are we talking?"

"I mean, he was still wearing a towel and all," the girl clarified. "It was just a little distracting to give a report while he was so...." She paused, waving her hand around as she searched for a word.

"Practically naked?" Ria offered.

Charise nodded. Ria couldn't help but laugh quietly at how much the prince had managed to fluster her shy shrine maiden. "Dear, I wouldn't assume Prince Darius meant anything by the way he behaved. I'm gathering very quickly that he's not the kind to overthink etiquette. Frankly I'm not sure he'd find himself wearing much of anything if he didn't have valets. I don't think he intends to be dressed or undressed, so much as he just happens to be one or the other at any given moment."

"Are you sure?" Charise looked skeptical.

"Trust me, Charise," the Oracle reassured her, "Darius has lived near the Aurora Shrine all of his life. He knows of the vows we take to keep our lives free of distractions that could conflict with our dedication to the Knights, and he respects them. He wouldn't purposely try to tempt you."

"If you say so." Charise paused, biting her lip before she went on. "Why did you have to send me though, Miss Ria? I'm no good at this kind of stuff! I babbled and I dropped things and I banged my knee and, well, not giving Prince Darius all of the information we found just made me a nervous wreck."

"Charise," Ria offered in a comforting tone, "even if Darius has begun to trust me more, he still sees me at odds with his father. If I had come to him suggesting General Riggs for the position outright, even with his impressive records, Magnus would encourage him to resist me on principle. You, on the other hand, were just doing your job. The information will seem less biased coming from you."

"But we both saw in the records that there were three or four more generals with records as good as General Riggs'. Maybe even a little better in some ways. We didn't give him all of the choices."

Ria nodded, smiling smugly at her young companion. "True. But none of those other choices were also the Knight-

Captain Elect."

Charise's eyes widened. The girl started to squeak, but Ria shushed her and led her out of the antechamber to the elevator platform before she could draw more attention.

Charise started again. "You're saying he's—"

Ria thrust her index finger up in front of her lips, signaling the girl to stay quiet. Though she trusted her shrine maidens, it was best that something this important be kept among as few minds as was possible. Charise practically bounced with anticipation as they rode down to the floor below and hurried to Ria's personal chambers.

Once the door was safely shut, Charise threw her hands in the air, nearly knocking her glasses off of her face in the process. "Why didn't you tell me that?"

"Are you saying that knowing would have made it easier?"

"Well," Charise thought for a moment. "Okay, no. But still! You're saying that General Riggs should have been the Knight-Captain? Won't that be, you know...." She trailed off, searching again.

"Wildly awkward?" Ria offered.

Charise nodded. "Yeah, that."

Ria looked down, returning the nod. "It's a possibility I've considered, yes. But Maxos is a man of great maturity and discipline. I have no doubt he'll endure the arrangement, even if it disappoints him. He has a different outlook on the world from that of most Vatrislanders. To him, everything happens for a reason. He'll hold to that outlook. He knows what's at stake."

Charise murmured her understanding. "But... there's still something I don't get. I see why you couldn't go, but you never explained why you sent me specifically to talk to him? I mean, there are other women here who are much more confident than I am. They could have done what I did without getting so out of sorts."

Ria sighed. She seated herself on the narrow bed draped with an old floral-patterned quilt and pointed across the room to an old fashioned desk. "There's a journal in the left drawer of that desk. Fetch it for me, would you?"

Charise crossed the warmly lit room and tugged open the drawer Ria had indicated. She returned to the bed with the weathered old book and held it out. Ria didn't accept the book, but instead just patted the other end of the bed. The girl sat beside her.

"Open to...hm." Ria looked toward the ceiling, lost for a moment reminiscing. "Goodness, anything during the summer, twenty-sixth year of King Kairus' reign ought to do it. Just pick a day and read."

The girl paged through to the appropriate section, picked a date and read aloud. "Another depressing day at Aurora Tower behind me. Today we had to sing hymns about our duty to the Knights and the Oracle. It's so embarrassing! I can't get out of the music hour even though everybody knows I sound like a sick duck when I sing. Some of the other girls even quacked when they passed me in the hall today. I should be studying for my diplomatic etiquette exam right now, but I just can't seem to focus. I just wish I could get out of here, but my parents seemed so happy when I said that I wanted to do this. I can't just quit and let them down, but I feel so out of place here. I don't know what to do."

The early days began to come back to Ria. "I felt more like a misfit than a maiden those first few months," she said, running her fingers over the quilt beneath them. "I used to tug this very quilt over my head when the morning wake up calls came. A few times I even tried to look as sick or as miserable as I could to see if I could get out of hymns."

"Did it work?" Charise asked.

Ria shook her head. "Rarely," she replied.

Charise looked back at the diary. "So you stuck it out for your parents then?"

"In part, yes," the Oracle answered. "But I really did come close to telling them I was through with it all a few times. Once, I even came home solely to break the news to them."

"What stopped you?"

Ria smirked. "An unintentional guilt trip. When I arrived, they had a surprise party waiting for me. They'd invited neighbors over, made cookies and cakes to celebrate for me. Father had even commissioned a painter to do a little portrait of me in my habit. Let's just say it seemed like a bad time to tell them I wanted to apprentice myself to an herbalist instead."

The two laughed quietly. "I never would have guessed, Miss Ria," Charise told her. "You just seem so confident. I can't imagine something getting to you."

"Well of course I'm confident now," Ria said, clearing her mind of those memories from so long ago. "You haven't read the part where it gets better. Let me see." She took the book and paged forward. The cheap paper had yellowed a bit at the outside edges, but otherwise, the journal had held up well during her years of sleep.

As she paged further from the incidents around that hard summer, she started to see more girlish doodles in the margins beside her words. A mountaintop and a cloud here. A deer there. These were the happier entries. She passed the book back to the younger shrine maiden. "Here, try this one from the winter."

"Oracle Celeste is awake again!" Charise read aloud. "She'll only be up and about for a day or two before she goes back to sleep, but she took some time to listen to me play the recorder she gave me in the fall. She says I have a natural talent for it, and by springtime, I might be able to play alongside the choir instead of singing. No more singing!" The girl laughed as she read the last line. "You seem so excited here."

"I was! I never liked music before that because of my voice," Ria continued, "but my Oracle helped me find my place.

Sure enough, it was the little push that I needed to become more confident. I started to succeed at things, and when I did, I would take on harder challenges. Slowly, I became the young woman whom Oracle Celeste would chose to take her place. It was an honor that I never could have imagined for myself when I began."

Charise nodded and said nothing, seeming to think it all over. Anytime the girl would get so quiet and compliant, Ria saw the hints of her young self that had brought Charise to her attention in the first place. She wondered if Oracle Celeste had seen something special in her when she'd comforted and encouraged a duck-voiced misfit. Had the knack she'd turned out to have for divination been a stroke of luck, or a nurtured effort? Ria regretted that there had been no reason for her Oracle to stay awake when she'd been young. She would have loved to know one of her most influential heroes better. At least now she could be around to give that very privilege to her own maidens.

"The challenges you face are going to grow whether you welcome them or not, Charise. I was able to start serving at the shrine during a time of peace, but you serve in a time of trouble. The Knights will face crises out in the field, and to further complicate things, we face resistance from the crown right here at home. I know that life here will be tough, yes, but as they say, 'no sword worth drawing is forged without fire.'" The Oracle rose from the bed, turned to the young maiden, and placed her hands on the girl's shoulders. "Embrace that fire, even if you can't yet imagine what it will make of you tomorrow."

Charise looked up into her mentor's eyes, offering a half-smile. She nudged her glasses up on her nose and stood. "I'll try, Oracle. I promise."

Ria just shook her head. "You know what? I think I've liked Miss Ria better so far. Why don't you stick with that?"

The girl nodded, and suddenly pulled Ria into a tight hug. For a moment, she tensed, having gone decades now without such an open display of affection, but quickly relaxed and wrapped the timid teenager in her arms. She hadn't thought in a long time about how her lifelong vow to be the Oracle of the Arms would not just deny her marriage, but also motherhood. Many maidens left after a number of years of service, after which they were no longer bound by their vows, but looking after her junior maidens was the closest she would ever get to having children of her own. A feeling of sincere gratitude for the opportunity to nurture and shape them overcame her, and she squeezed the girl in her arms all the more.

"Now," Ria whispered, letting the girl go and patting her cheek. "I know you pushed yourself today. If Prince Darius responded to the information you gave him the way you say he did, then you've done more than your fair share. Go on and get some rest. I'll want you wide awake and sharp tomorrow as we see our Knight off at the stables."

"Yes, Miss Ria. Have a good night." Charise stepped away, now warmly smiling, and slipped out the door.

The Oracle found herself unable to stop smiling too as she readied herself for bed. The fires she'd prepared Charise for tonight would certainly come, but she, her maidens, and the Knights would face them boldly.

6

For the second day in a row, Darius found himself up earlier than usual to be buckled into his armor by attendants. Once fully clad, he hefted the Titangavel up onto his shoulder and made swiftly to exit his room. A storm brewed in the northwestern sky, and he'd have to ride quickly if he were to have any hope of not spending a whole day soaking wet. He hoped that the stable master had fully prepped Comet, his riding hound, as he tugged open the door into the hallway.

"Ah, perfect timing!"

Magnus stood before him, fist raised as though he'd been prepared to knock. Darius raised his eyebrows. He hadn't really wanted to speak further to his father before he left, preferring to get out to the Cryptwastes and let his actions speak for themselves. He managed to push some words out as he stepped past and started on his way down the hall. "Hello father. Didn't expect to see you before I left."

Magnus caught up and matched his son's stride, continuing with his sociable, warm facade. "I'm glad I caught you then. I noticed the shrine maidens removing one of the Aurora Arms from the tower this morning. I take it you've chosen your second?"

Darius tightened his lips. He'd sent word to Aurora Tower before sunrise to have Watchward brought down and packed for his journey in hopes of avoiding unwanted attention. Apparently, nothing on the castle grounds slipped by his father. "I've got it narrowed down," he replied flatly.

When he didn't speak further, Magnus prodded, "Well don't keep me in suspense, boy! Who are we looking at?"

For a moment, Darius considered resisting his father's prying, but he ultimately relented. There was no point in starting a fight right before he got on the road. If he did, it might only delay him. "If you must know, I'll be giving a weapon to one of your generals. I'm thinking General Maxos Riggs. He's got a great record."

Magnus winced. "Really? Riggs? Aren't you overlooking the best man for the job?"

Darius was torn. Half of his mind was curious about what his father had to say. The other half balked, offended. As if he couldn't make this decision on his own. He hadn't asked for help. He had to remind himself that he could still make whatever call he wanted in the field before he let curiosity get the better of him. "Go on."

"Another of my generals, Lief Andler, is a much better fit," Magnus stated plainly.

"Because?"

"Riggs is a fine general and has served me well, but Andler's record is just as good, and he has a wife and two kids right here in Cloudbreach. He'll better understand your priorities to the crown. Give you fewer arguments. Riggs married himself a H'tyanni, and she's got family across the border. He might not have his whole heart with us."

"Hmm," Darius acknowledged. It seemed like such a small thing. Relations between Vatrisland and the coastal H'tyanni Empire weren't hostile. The two nations just generally tried to stay out of one another's business. Their shared border was comprised almost entirely of lands in the Cryptwastes, so there was little worth contesting. Still, he had hoped for something more concrete than cultural tensions to guide him.

"Well, don't you agree?"

Darius shrugged, "Look, I'll add him to my list, but I'd still like to talk to both of them in person before I make my call."

Magnus laughed and shook his head, a hint of condescension in his voice. "Son, don't you think I know my generals well enough to tell you who's best for this? Really..."

"Well, I'd still like to see for myself, father," the prince countered. He hadn't intended to sound so defiant when he had said it, but his annoyance crept through.

"Okay, Okay." Magnus trailed off just long enough to let him think the issue was closed. "But if I can't trust you on this issue, I'm not sure if I can trust you with the parting gift I had set aside."

Darius halted. They had come to a stop right in the middle of the grand entrance hall. He was a short walk from the castle's front doors, and from there, not much farther to the royal stables where Comet waited, no doubt eager as he always was once they saddled him. He didn't doubt that his father had withheld this reversal for the very last minute just in case, and he cursed his curiosity for stopping him now.

He steeled his will. "This isn't the kind of thing where you can just buy me, father. I'm the Knight-Captain of the Aurora Knights. I have to use my own judgment."

"Of course, of course," the king went on, "but the records show them both to be equal in nearly every other way. What's wrong with settling your choice now? Especially when it could mean the difference between a week riding on the back of a wet, filthy mongrel, and arriving at Fort Diligence in the Cryptwastes this very night."

Father couldn't mean it. There was only one thing his father could give him to keep that promise, and it would indeed be too good a gift to pass up.

"You're kidding."

"Am I?"

"The Relentless?"

Magnus smiled. "Your flight out to the Cryptwastes could be her maiden voyage. Think, Darius, about how quickly you could react to the demands of your position with her. At best, your hound would bear you there in six days, maybe five. The Relentless will have you there by supper."

Darius eyed the castle doors. The part of him that wished he'd just kept walking straight out the door was rapidly shrinking beside the part that imagined having the largest skyship the world had ever known at his command. He'd idled away more than a few hours each month watching the thing go from frame to hull, hull to vessel, and vessel to glorious magecraft flagship. No doubt his father had noticed his fascination, and had filed away that knowledge for just the right time.

One tiny decision, and he could have this tool at his command. How critical was it really that he interview the two generals? How much more good would he be able to do if he had The Relentless to carry the Knights around the world in a fraction of the time it would take a mount to do the same?

It would be foolish to let this slip by. There was too much to lose. Though he didn't look his father in the eye, Darius nodded, "General Andler will be honored to hear he's been chosen to serve at my side."

"That's my boy!" Magnus shouted, clapping a hand on his son's armored shoulder. "I knew you had a good head on your shoulders. Come! I've had them put a finish on her suitable for a prince."

The two turned away from the castle's front doors, and away from the stable where Comet would be unsaddled and sent back to his pen. Instead, they walked deeper into the castle, toward the magecraft labs and the hangar where The Relentless awaited.

XXX

68

The Relentless was far and away the most glorious device of modern magecraft ever imagined. It rested in its hangar on two sturdy steel skids, each of which housed a long shaft of fiery yellow enchanted crystal capable of propelling the vessel into the sky. Its angular, sleek wooden frame gave it the appearance of moving even as it stood still, towering over the Oracle and Charise, who had joined Darius and his father. Junior craftsmen studied the vessel from all angles, some walking along the deck on top, others examining the crystals that would propel it into the sky for a last minute triple-check.

The Oracle gaped at it, her typical restraint failing her. Charise stood beside her, torn between matching her superior's expression and watching out for busy craftsmen racing this way and that. Maybe his father had gone a little overboard decking the entire vessel from tip to tail with the colors and crest of Vatrisland.

"Prince Darius," the Oracle managed, "are you certain this doesn't send something of a...mixed message regarding the Knights' priorities?"

Looking at it himself, Darius really did struggle to justify the biased spectacle that The Relentless represented, but he tried his best. "Hey, this is the first time one of the Knights has actually come directly from royal blood, you know? It would be wasteful not to harness the resources that a kingdom's ruler freely offers. Think of how much faster we'll get around in this thing."

The Oracle furrowed her brow, looking skeptical.

"You wished to see me, My Lord?" a sharp feminine voice called across the hangar.

The brilliant, gorgeous Vasna Hain, head of magecraft research and development for Vatrisland approached, her calf-high black boots issuing business-like clicks with each step. She swept through the groups of busy workers without so much as a moment's hesitation in her stride, the tails of her black double-breasted long coat and volumes of curly red hair trailing out behind her. Darius couldn't resist looking her over. Her confidence commanded his attention every time she came near him.

"Indeed, Miss Hain!" Magnus replied, stepping to her side. "I suppose there are some introductions in order. Of course, you already know of my son, Darius."

She crossed one arm over her chest and bowed. "Prince Darius. Congratulations on your recent appointment as Knight-Captain."

Darius only nodded, taken off guard by her formality. They'd rarely interacted face-to-face. He'd watched her from afar at times when he'd come to view The Relentless, and she'd always carried herself with such self-assurance that it somehow unnerved him to have her treat him as a superior.

"And this is our Oracle of the Arms. Come down to see our pride and joy here. Isn't that right?"

The two women shook hands. "This is quite a vessel you've come up with, Miss Hain. I've never seen anything like it," added the Oracle.

The king cut off the breath Vasna took in to respond, "Of course it's quite a vessel! I'd expect nothing less from my little magecraft prodigy here." He paused for a moment to ruffle her tricorn hat. "Came all the way down from the mages' college out in Summerpoint to serve me here. Been worth her weight in gold, too. Well, go on my dear! No need to be humble. Tell her how it works!"

Vasna straightened her hat, cleared her throat, and beckoned for the group to follow her closer to the looming ship. "The two large crystals you see here at the bottom evoke a combination of heat and force, levitating the vessel. That output can be moderated for each crystal individually by a focused spellcaster from the helm position on the bridge to make the ship accelerate, slow down, or bank for turns as needed."

"Won't that exhaust a pilot quickly?" Charise piped up.

The four turned to look at her. She wrung her hands and stammered to explain herself. "I mean, I see the other girls at the tower. The ones w-who are good at casting spells and stuff. That kind of thing seems to tire them out pretty quickly."

Vasna nodded in affirmation, addressing the others. "Actually, the girl's right. We have six or so, myself included, who can pilot the ship for perhaps an hour at a time before needing rest. It takes a regular rotation to keep her in the air, but on a few test flights up into the peaks, we've all gotten pretty good and handing off the effort one crystal at a time."

The group walked around to the front of the ship and into it by way of an extended ramp. Vasna continued narrating her tour as she walked magelamp-lit hallways of warm-toned wood. "She sleeps thirty comfortably, and that includes six private cabins for special guests and the like. We need a minimum of five active crew to have her in motion, so we can keep several shifts in rotation if we have to fly overnight."

Vasna stopped briefly next to one of the private cabins and pushed the door open, gesturing for Darius to peek in. It was a little smaller than his bath chamber at the castle, with a narrow bed and closet space for his armor and perhaps a few changes of clothing and some personal items. Nothing fancy, but he was pleased that he'd have more space to himself than most of the hammock-bound crew.

They continued through the halls and up a staircase. "And this," she said as they entered the next room, "is the bridge." An array of large windows at the front of the wide room gave the group a view of the hangar and the mountains and sky beyond the huge sliding doors. Within the room, two crewmen moved from station to station, bantering and arguing with one another as they checked on the wide variety of humming, glowing, magical devices that would contribute to keeping the ship aloft. Upon seeing their audience, the lanky one of the two crewmen tugged brass rimmed goggles upward, letting them rest on his forehead where they lifted his wild brown hair away from his eyes. He approached Vasna and the others with long strides, calling out in a slow, deep voice, "Hey Captain." Then he slapped an open palm into Darius' hand and gave it a vigorous shake. "Hey, welcome aboard, buddy."

"Treve!" called out the other shorter crewman, "Treve, that's the prince!"

Treve squinted, "You sure, Pierce? He looks like some kinda captain of the guard or something."

"Your friend has it right," Darius confirmed, chuckling as he did. He warmly returned the handshake without missing a beat. Rarely did anyone outside of his military squad treat him like a normal human being. Between a lifetime of royal tradition and becoming an Aurora Knight, it was a refreshing change of pace to not be fawned over.

"Oh, sorry about that, Your Lordship!" Treve bowed his head while still shaking the prince's hand. "I spend a lot of time in the hangar here. They all tell me I need to get out more."

Before Darius could reassure the crewman, his shorter companion approached, running a hand over his perfectly parted hair as he did. He bowed formally with an arm crossed over his middle. "Pierce DeLangere, Your Majesty. It will be an honor to serve aboard your flagship."

The other added, "Oh, and uh, Trevor Graves. Everyone calls me Treve though, so feel free."

Vasna further introduced them. "Pierce and Treve are part of the piloting rotation for The Relentless. What they lack in a broad spellcasting education, they more than make up in a focused apprenticeship in magecraft and power channeling."

Darius nodded. "I look forward to seeing each of you in action at the helm. If you have Miss Hain's trust with her baby here, you've got mine too." Both crewmen smiled at his words of approval.

"Well," Vasna went on, "that's about all there is to it. We're making final preparations as we speak. We'll be ready to take off shortly, so I'll leave you to take care of any last minute business." She bowed her head before beckoning her assistants to follow her back into the halls of the ship.

Magnus beamed as he looked out at the open sky beyond the hangar doors, "This is it then, boy. Don't let me down now. With The Relentless at your command, you and your Knights can spread the glory of Vatrisland across the world." He turned and clasped Darius' shoulder with one hand, looking into his eyes. The prince didn't feel pride in his father's gaze, but rather expectation. "Use her to strike awe into your allies and fear into your enemies. For Vatrisland!"

"For Vatrisland," Darius echoed. At the edge of his vision, The Oracle clenched her lips together tightly enough to split a walnut. Magnus must have noticed as well. One end of the king's mouth was turned up in a subtle half-smile. The whole display left him feeling like a pawn, but he didn't dare question his father in public. Memories of Magnus striking him for mouthing off as a child never seemed to completely lose their grip on him no matter how often he told himself he was a grown man now.

"That's a good lad." His father patted his shoulder one last time before facing Ria. "I suppose we should make sure we don't delay their launch any further, hm?"

"I suppose not," she responded. At that she turned to Darius. "Fight well, Prince Vatri. Assemble and lead your Knights wisely. We will all hope for your victory and safe return." Her voice didn't waver, but he could see the worry in her eyes. Still, he thanked her, and she left the bridge with the king and Charise.

When he felt certain they were all out of earshot, he leaned against the wall and sighed loudly. Any hope that he could go even one day without facing the mounting pressure and scrutiny from his father and the Oracle was rapidly fading. He'd always imagined the leader of the Aurora Knights to be free; a man able to react to trouble at a moment's notice guided by his own judgment. For him, it would instead be a life of two sides tugging so hard that they might rip him in two.

At least, he comforted himself, neither of them would be with him out in the field. Maybe now he'd get a chance to make some decisions of his own free will.

"I know you are doing your best."

Darius snapped away from the wall, startled by the Oracle's voice. It seemed to come from inside of his head.

"Don't worry," her voice continued. "As long as you have the Titangavel with you, we can communicate from a distance like this. Just envision yourself speaking with me as you talk and I'll hear you. In this way, I can offer you support in battle if you provide me with information about your foes and challenges in the field."

So this was how her voice had seemed so close when he'd been training against the summoned creatures the other day. Darius glanced around again to make sure none of the crew would be around to see him looking as though he were talking to himself, but before he could respond, another voice interrupted.

"Darius? Are you still on the bridge, boy?" his father bellowed from nearby.

Darius spotted a glow emanating from one of the stations on the bridge. Mounted into a sturdy wooden stand was a magic mirror like the ones in Aurora Tower.

"Yes?" Darius didn't approach the mirror, but instead just yelled across the cabin, failing to hide the agitation in his voice.

"Ah, good! Just giving this a try from the hangar. The Relentless is well equipped for communication, as you can see. I'll make sure to keep in touch every day or so. Don't hesitate to contact me if you're having trouble making a decision. I'll be happy to point you in the right direction."

Darius clenched his eyes shut and slumped backward against the wall again, thumping the back of his head against it in frustration a few times for good measure. The Oracle's voice sounded again, "Darius, can you hear me? Is there something wrong?"

"Just debating the merits of mutiny," the prince grumbled.

"What was that?" the two voices asked back in perfect unison.

"Nothing!" Darius sighed. "Nothing at all."

7

Ria looked on nervously as The Relentless, shining with Vatrisland's proud heraldry, rose into the air, propelled by the massive shafts of crystal beneath it that hummed and glowed with carefully harnessed magical power. The flagship slipped carefully out of the hangar doors to the applause of the hardworking magecraft technicians who had toiled to make Vasna's design a reality, and sped northward into the sky.

Her influence on Darius would be diminished from afar, but so would Magnus'. Though both had ways to stay in touch with the prince from a distance, he would be making his own decisions in the heat of the moment now. The thought made Ria nervous. Darius had a strong sense of honor and a desire to do good, but the king's power over him would remain an unpredictable element.

"You're welcome, by the way."

Ria turned. Sure enough, Magnus had sauntered up to her. He wore the smug smile and relaxed gaze of a man with everything under his control. His presumptuous conversation starter only needled her further, but she tucked her head to him and kept up appearances in public. "King Magnus."

The king hesitated for a moment, leaving her an opening to thank him. When she didn't give him the pleasure, he just laughed and chided her, "Really, Oracle? Here I've gone and put the greatest, most ingenious magecraft vehicle ever built into service for the Aurora Knights, and you can't get over yourself long enough to thank me? Does it really set a good example for the young, impressionable shrine maiden to be so bitter?"

Ria pressed her lips together. Though the king made his point with a certain intolerable superiority, in the end, he was right. How could she hope for the girls and women in her service to act with grace and humility if she couldn't do so herself? She found the self-control to resist sighing loudly before she answered him. "You're right, Your Majesty. Forgive me. Your gift will be a great aid to the Knights, and I do thank you."

"That's better," he said, drawing out his words patronizing smarm as he spoke. "I know we've had our differences, Oracle, but in the end, we really are on the same team."

"Oh?" the Oracle asked, keeping her tone pleasant.

"Of course," the king went on. He began to walk across the hangar back toward the castle proper as he spoke. Ria kept up at his side, with Charise trailing not far behind. "We're on Darius' team. We both want to see the boy make wise decisions with the tools we've given him. We're both guiding him. Depending on him. Even placing our highest hopes in him."

He was lying, of course. Magnus was on his own team. She offered her own take on it as diplomatically as she could. "I would love to see your son make wise decisions, King Magnus, but in the end, isn't wisdom in the eye of the beholder? One man's wisdom is another's stubbornness. The definition itself depends upon what those high hopes for him are."

The king just laughed again. "Oh, Oracle. It's never enough for you is it? You can't just say 'of course, Your Majesty,' and let things be. You must set yourself at odds with me every chance you get."

"Your Majesty," she stated firmly, "I'm just reminding you that my position is clear. The Aurora Knights are to be a force in defense of the entire world. I'll not see them made the pawns of a single nation, whether officially or otherwise."

"Pawns? Really? Don't you think you overestimate your control of the Knights?" His voice had shifted from that patronizing tone to something more intimidating, just above a whisper. He circled around in front of her and the two came to a stop in a statuary hall. Mid-morning sunlight poured in through towering, arched windows, playing over the stoic statues of Vatrisland's past kings. Ria suddenly felt very small, surrounded by the proud rulers who had raised the mountainous nation to greatness. No doubt he'd stopped her in such an intimidating place on purpose.

"Think about it, Oracle. We both know Darius makes his own binding decisions as Knight-Captain. You cannot forbid him from making a choice with which you disagree. If he should decide to recruit a team of patriots who would come to aid their king and homeland first, what could you do to stop him? You should be as afraid of the Knights' power as I used to be."

A chill ran up the back of Ria's neck. "Used to be?" she echoed.

He brought his voice back up to its former volume, flashing her a cunning smile. "My son is showing a lot of wisdom lately, Oracle. He understood the value of having The Relentless at his command. He was happy to take it too, in exchange for agreeing to some fatherly guidance on choosing his second-in-command."

So The Relentless hadn't just been a parting gift from father to son. Ria hardened her expression at Magnus. "Leverage," she murmured.

Magnus flashed a confident smile. "You didn't think I would just give the boy my ship, did you? There's far too much at stake here to leave anything to chance, my dear. Don't worry, though. General Andler is a mighty and capable fighter, and has his priorities straight, too. He'll encourage Darius to make wise decisions."

Ria stood still. If Darius followed through on his father's

wishes, Magnus would have the first two Aurora Knights under his thumb. She felt the warm hand of Charise on her back, bracing her from behind. Only then did she realize that she'd grown unsteady.

"You're looking unwell, Oracle," Magnus mocked. "Why don't you go get some rest? I'll keep an eye on Darius and make sure everything comes together just right." The king left the two women in the statuary. As he rounded the corner to exit the room, Ria could have sworn she saw an extra spring in the old snake's step.

The same worst-case scenarios that had worried her the night Ria had agreed to let Magnus choose the leader of the Knights now swam through her mind again. Her ears rang and sounds seemed muffled, as though she were underwater. A faint call of "Oracle" fought to break through haunting images of five Knights, all bearing Vatrisland's standard and heraldry at the head of a mighty army.

"Oracle?"

"Miss Ria, are you okay?"

The last call dispelled the images that plagued her. Charise touched her shoulder, anchoring her back in the real. She set her feet, and felt steady again. "Yes. Yes, I think so. I'm sorry."

"What do we do first? We have to do something."

She turned face Charise. The girl frowned with worry, but Ria detected something else from her, too. There was no paralysis about her, like there had been when they'd first met.

"I don't think I know," Ria confessed. Her instinct was to call out to Darius through the Titangavel, to counsel him and try to change his mind, but what would she say? He was the kind of man to keep his word, and she'd set things up so that he wouldn't know she'd had a hand in picking General Riggs. She would look as manipulative as Magnus to him if she admitted she'd deceived him now, and that would only drive him further into his father's influences.

Charise took a deep breath and blew it out. She looked back at Ria steadily. "Miss Ria, you said there would be fire. I'm afraid, but I won't just let him treat you like that without doing something. Whatever you need from me, I'm ready."

Ria marveled at Charise. Had the girl really taken her advice to heart so quickly? Words were one thing, but taking action would be the real test.

Ria thought back to her teenage years. Maybe she too had risen to meet her challenges that quickly once she'd been given sincere encouragement. The memory lifted her spirits.

"Okay," she concluded with a nod. "Let's get to fighting through that fire."

XXX

The two women took a table to share in the top chamber of Aurora Tower and spread out General Andler's public records alongside two cups and a kettle of hot tea. The general's record was impressive for sure. He had numerous victories to his name, in combat against both foreign rebels and against monsters that had menaced the Vatrisland countryside. He was so highly decorated that Ria envisioned him tipping to one side under the weight of his medals.

"Maybe he won't be so bad as a Knight," Charise offered, sipping at her teacup as she pawed through the documents spread out before her. "I mean, he seems really competent."

Ria shook her head, pressing her lips tightly together for a moment in concentration. "And maybe King Magnus is really a generous man who made a decision with the world's best interests at heart," Ria replied, raising a skeptical eyebrow.

Charise got the point. She went back to digging through the records.

Ria got back to her search as well. Though Andler's whole

file made her uncomfortable, the comments from his superiors on his promotions and decorations troubled her even more. There were plenty of standard remarks about his loyalty to the kingdom, but the praise heaped on him in spite of the extensive losses his units would take in combat disturbed her. Many high generals, as well as King Magnus, had left comments justifying the losses and praising Andler's resulting fast mission execution. It was the kind of philosophy that could result in both lost Knights and lost Aurora Arms.

What bothered her even more, though, was the degree to which she had been broadsided by Magnus that day. She could see that she'd been cocky to assume her simple plan could be set into motion and left to come about without any further care. Now the King's sneering face taunted her in her mind. She couldn't hope to compete against a gift like The Relentless with only the offerings that the Aurora Shrine brought in. The Knights had drifted from the minds of the people in the recent decades of relative peace, and giving had dwindled, tightening their budget.

"Oracle?" Charise prodded her.

"Yes?"

"You're, uh, crinkling the records."

Ria looked down and unclenched her fist, letting the papers go. She leaned back in her chair, sighing as she rubbed her face and wrung her hands, trying to relax them. "It's so frustrating to be outfoxed by him. Here I told myself that could deal with whatever he threw at me, and he's ended up getting everything he's wanted since day one."

Charise frowned in sympathy.

Ria tilted her head back to stare at the ceiling. "I need some way to get a step ahead of him," she murmured, "or we're going to have the most memorable team of Aurora Knights in history, and not in a good way either."

Charise allowed the silence to hang for a moment before

she hesitantly replied, "What if someone warned you about what was coming?"

"As nice as that would be, we don't have anyone in the castle loyal enough to us to do that."

"I could do it."

Ria sat back upright in her chair. Charise wasn't looking at her. The girl kept her eyes fixed downward at the table as she absentmindedly scribbled on a stray piece of blank paper in front of her. The Oracle looked around the chamber. Rarely since she'd awoken had she seen the room empty, but at that moment, it was vacant except for the two of them.

She turned back to the girl and lowered her voice. "Charise, I cannot ask you to do that. What if you were found out? Even with the sway I have, I wouldn't be able to protect you if you were found guilty of treason."

"I know that," the girl replied quietly, "but don't you really believe that something awful is out there in the Cryptwastes? I mean, you wouldn't have started assembling the Knights if you hadn't thought that it was something really important, right?"

Ria pursed her lips and scowled. She could see where this was going but everything within her told her to resist. "Charise, I don't think you understand the gravity of what you're offering to do. King Magnus won't hesitate to have you executed if he catches you spying."

The teen nodded her head, still staring at her paper and doodling. "If that necromancer is as dangerous as you say, though, then the whole world's safety is at stake. Imagine if the Knights refuse to protect nations that won't swear fealty to King Magnus, or worse still, fight only for Vatrisland. How could risking one shrine maiden not be worth it?"

Was this the same girl she'd met the evening that she'd woken up from her sleep? How was this timid, flustered novice now deftly carving through her every objection? Ria struggled to stay firm on the issue. "Charise, we will find another way to do this. I'm not going to put in that position."

"Oracle." Charise finally looked up as she spoke clearly. "Aren't we called to do whatever it takes? It's what our hymns say. 'In greatest need, and darkest hour,' right? You've got to admit that this qualifies."

Ria just stared back at the girl, now fully disarmed.

"All of my life I've been underestimated," she went on. "Nobody ever asked much of me because they didn't think I had any gifts, but this is the one time that I'm the perfect person to get something done. Who's going to suspect the quiet, nervous bookworm to be a spy? King Magnus already behaves like I don't exist when we're around him, and you've had me fetch things from the castle library more than a few times now, so the staff are already used to seeing me in the halls."

The Oracle looked down. All that she had left were selfish, emotional arguments. Maybe all of the long years she'd spent in that meditative sleep had left her starved for human attachment. In just two days, she'd already become so attached to Charise. They'd needed one another. Ria couldn't help but remember how she'd always thought of Oracle Celeste as the giver in their friendship. Perhaps her own mentor had felt the same way about her as she now did about Charise.

Ria sighed, accepting her defeat. "Can you at least promise me that you'll be careful? I have enough trouble keeping Darius in line. I don't want to have to worry about you too."

Charise pressed her lips together and nodded. "I'll try to not do anything too risky."

Ria stood and managed to push out a laugh in hopes of breaking the tension. She squeezed the girl on the shoulder, saying, "Don't just try, okay? Succeed."

Charise smiled and nodded. "Well, if we've gotten everything we need out of all of this, I'll get it all together and run it back to the castle, where I have some research to do this very afternoon." She winked as she finished.

"How studious! I won't keep you then," the Oracle concluded with a smile.

Charise set about clearing the table and putting the documents back in order. With her pupil's attention occupied, Ria peered out of the corner of her eye at the girl's notes, curious to see what she'd been scribbling so intently as they'd talked.

On the note sheet, alongside notes from General Andler's record, was a small, coin-sized drawing of a campfire. A playful, carefree doodle of round simple logs coming together like spokes on a wheel supported a bouncy looking tongue of flame.

Ria turned away and headed toward her quarters with a happy smile spreading across her face.

8

The Relentless now cruised high over the Vatrisland countryside, covering the miles between Cloudbreach and the Cryptwastes at a steady clip. Darius couldn't help looking down out of the windows as the world passed by beneath them. They were far to the north of the capital now, away from the mountains and needle-clad trees, and coming to the end of the fertile farmlands of central Vatrisland. He could hardly imagine the reactions of people looking into the late afternoon sky, seeing something so large fly past them so smoothly. There would be plenty of skeptical looks shot across Vatrisland's farmers' supper tables tonight as family members shared the strange sight with one another.

He pried himself away from the view at the window to look around the bridge. Treve stood at the helm. A gentle glow emitted from his hands as he subtly drew them back and forth over a pair of slender crystals mounted at his station. The ship banked gently in the direction of whichever crystal he eased away from, and leveled out as he evened his efforts again. Unlike Vasna and Pierce, however, who both remained quite still during the process, Treve bobbed his head rhythmically, humming melodies from old Vatrisland folk tunes as he steered the craft. Darius made a note to get to know the man better. He suspected they'd get along well.

"I used to scold him for doing that, you know," Vasna said, sliding up alongside the prince with her arms crossed. "Told him it was distracting the rest of the crew, and to knock it off. Turns out he doesn't fly as well when he can't do it, and his average is better than most casters' best efforts, so we learned to love it."

"Is he as good as you are?" Darius asked.

"At least. Probably better." Then she added quietly, "It's irked me ever since I noticed it. If he knows it, he doesn't brag about it or anything, though."

The prince chuckled softly. "So you're a little competitive then?"

She tugged her coat, smoothing out a wrinkle, and looked at him with a perfectly straight face. "Always," she said. "I did not earn such a prestigious position by being lax with myself."

Darius crossed his arms and leaned against the wall. "That's right. Father did drop the word 'prodigy' when he described you."

Vasna murmured an agreement as she peeked over another crewman's shoulder at his station. After a moment, she nodded at what she saw and continued. "Graduated at the top of my class from the academy at Summerpoint. Achieved a Grand Master's in magecraft two years ahead of my peers. Was hand-selected by your father's recruiter and proceeded to improve the output and efficiency of every magecraft device put in front of me for the next four years. And that was on the side while I designed and oversaw the construction of The Relentless by day."

She certainly was wound up tight. Darius tried to lighten the mood once more. "And you're humble too, right?"

No luck. She shot him that perfectly serious look again. "Why should I be? I'm not even thirty and I've catapulted an entire kingdom ahead of the curve in both convenience and warfare. My work has redefined modernity. I leave our neighbors salivating with envy at Vatrisland's quality of life. I have plenty to be proud of, and plenty more to accomplish."

Darius was lost for words. He glanced around the bridge. The crewmen carried on without missing a beat. Apparently this was the status quo working with Vasna Hain. No wonder his father liked her so much. Perhaps The Relentless was named after her. It certainly fit.

The silence was broken by Pierce, who manned an observation post keeping watch for flying predators made curious about The Relentless. "Captain Hain, we're coming up on the Cryptwastes now."

Darius and Vasna both stepped toward the side windows of the bridge. The grassy plains had given way to scrubbier plant life as they'd flown. Further ahead lay only hills of cracked, bone-white dirt dotted with rocks and ruins.

The Cryptwastes had once been the Itradi Empire, a powerful nation that bordered Vatrisland to the north. The Itradi had rivaled Darius' ancestors in power and wealth for several hundred years prior to the forging of the Aurora Arms. The creation of the Arms, however, had inspired Vatrisland's people to a golden age of innovation and a proud military tradition. The Itradi had responded by starting a campaign of aggressive invention and development in a bid to keep up.

Competition between the two nations grew more and more fierce until the fateful day of the Blightfire. Historians were only be able to speculate on what caused the life-consuming wave of violet flame that blasted outward from Anceda Pryta, the Itradi capital. The wave had raced over a hundred miles in all directions, disintegrating every living thing it touched. Trees and plants were wholly reduced to dust. Men and animals left behind only their skeletons, which shortly thereafter rose up and wandered the land in mindless malice. Though buildings of wood in the less wealthy parts of the empire were reduced to ruins, curious explorers and looters would later discover that buildings in the capital had been left mostly untouched, owing to an Itradi love of stone construction. The towering royal ziggurat thought to be the exact center of the blast, still stood at the middle of the abandoned city,

87

eerily silent save for the shuffling bones of its former inhabitants.

The region had remained a wild land of roaming undead until about four hundred years ago, when another king from Darius' family line had ordered that the region be annexed into Vatrisland's borders and that forts be built around the perimeter. A few nearby nations had put up minimal protest to the effort, but they eventually backed down. Vatrisland really was the only nation with a large enough army to undertake containing the undead alongside its own defense, and once the number of undead escaping into neighboring nations dropped off, nobody argued with the results. From that time forward, the Cryptwastes had been surrounded and patrolled by Vatrisland's army, and occasionally explored by well-guarded expeditions in search of knowledge and relics to return to the king.

This was a new, more dangerous Cryptwaste though, Darius reminded himself. Scattered, disorganized undead were not so hard to fight off and manage. Legions of skeletons and mummified horrors all driven by the will of one man would be a different story. The tireless masses would now fight as one, and that would multiply their power considerably.

"There," Pierce said, pointing into the distance. "Fort Diligence is coming into view."

Darius spied it on the horizon as well. It was the most well-maintained of the forts surrounding the Cryptwastes due to its southernmost location, making it the last station between the ruined region and the towns of central Vatrisland. That said, the gray stone walls still looked remarkably weathered, as though they'd been lashed with wind carrying the bone-white dust that now clung to them like paste. The buildings within had fared better. Clean red banners bearing his homeland's mountain lion crest flapped in the wind whipping past the tall command center. The shorter barracks buildings only peeked the highest tips of their roofs over the wall from his high vantage point in The Relentless.

The skyship finally closed in and crested the wall of the fort to reveal hundreds of men gathered in uniform rows below. No doubt word had been sent ahead warning them to prepare for the prince's arrival, but Darius suspected that not everything had been clear. As the troops took in the size of The Relentless, they started to backpedal to make more room for the vessel to land. Either word of the ship's dimensions had not been sent, or the commanding officers had assumed that some exaggeration had been involved.

Darius looked at Vasna out of the corner of his eye. She grinned smugly, relishing the reactions.

The crew executed the vessel's landing with the yard with the clockwork precision only natural for a team trained by Vasna Hain. She, Darius, and the bridge crew strode through the halls of the ship down to the lower hatch to disembark. The troops outside had managed to reestablish rank and file by the time the ramp came down, and greeted the group with a salute. "Hail! Prince Vatri!" Their boots snapped together in perfect unison.

It was Darius' turn to grin. Though he found himself standing in a desolate wasteland far from his home in the capital, he was surrounded now by disciplined, honest men driven by Vatrisland's fighting spirit. This was his world, away from the throne rooms and forums, the lairs of silver-tongued dealers and backstabbers. That same sense of belonging he'd felt back among his squadmates in Cloudbreach stirred within him again.

From the front row of soldiers, a heavyset officer in ceremonial armor stepped forward, smoothing back his thinning gray hair as he did. Darius recognized the man, High General Draad, having seen him at a number of functions at the castle in years past.

"Prince Vatri, welcome to Fort Diligence," he said, offering a slight bow as he spoke. "It's an honor to have you here, both as Prince of Vatrisland and as the Knight-Captain of the Aurora

Knights."

"Thank you, High General," Darius replied. "Your men are looking well. If they're as tough and organized as they look, Vatrisland has nothing to be afraid of from this necromancer and his forces in the wastes."

Draad dismissed the men and they scattered to their various tasks around the base. Darius introduced Vasna to the high general as captain of The Relentless and (as she was quick to unsubtly remind him) its brilliant inventor. Together, the three toured the fort, and Darius found himself impressed by the operations that contained the horrors of the Cryptwastes. Vatrisland's military always performed well, but here, that quality extended into even the finest details of each soldier's efforts. Those manning the watchtowers stood at attention as still as statues. Men drilling in the central yard practiced with intense zeal, as though their exercises were in real battles.

Darius mentioned his observation to the high general as they watched clusters of men skirmish beneath the purple evening sky, and the older man nodded. "We need all of the discipline we can muster to stay strong in the face of the undead," he said. "When you wound a man, he might cower or retreat, but you can take the legs clean off of a walking corpse, and it'll keep crawling toward you without a second thought. Every time new troops are assigned here to reinforce us, they have to learn how to fight all over again, how to ruin a body so bad that it can't keep coming. It's a lot of extra work to drop each one."

"Mm," Darius grunted. He had been so caught up in his own transition to Knighthood that he hadn't considered the nature of his first foes. While he didn't doubt that the Titangavel's might and regenerative powers would give him a substantial upper hand, these soldiers wouldn't be so well-equipped. He watched as some of them lashed out at dummies with their spellblades, commanding their weapons to produce a magical burst of force as they landed

90

their blows. Vasna's weapon designs gave them an edge for sure, but behind those magic blades were still only mortal men with flaws and fears.

Darius needed to get down to the business of knighting his second-in-command if they were going to have hope of driving back their enemy. "High General, is General Andler drilling his troops out here right now?"

"Sure is. He's that one, right there." Draad pointed across the field at a man wearing a general's insignia. A cluster of Andler's troops worked their way through a series of obstacles nearby. One of the men lay on the ground in the shadow of General Andler clutching his knee and wincing in pain.

"Get up," the bald general commanded coldly.

"I can't, sir." The soldier struggled to speak through clenched teeth.

Andler maintained a stony scowl, raising his voice slightly and popping every hard consonant. "I don't care. And you know who else doesn't care? The damned don't care. And if you're a waste of skin like this on the battlefield, they'll claw your guts right out of your coward belly. Now get. Up."

Even from his position several yards away, Darius could see color drain from the soldier's sweaty face. The man rolled over and struggled to his feet, gingerly testing his weight on his injured leg. He pushed himself into a jog toward the next obstacle for only a moment before he dropped again in pain, not making a sound but mouthing swears as he squinted back tears in his eyes.

General Andler turned red, his flushed face highlighting a jagged scar along his cheek as he began to yell. "Who let this whining little girl into my army of real Vatrislanders? You put on a sorry display like this out there and you know what they'll do to you? They'll eat your yellow throat out! They'll eat it and then that blighter will make you into one of them!"

The soldier's face further contorted in shame and agony.

Andler's merciless tirade continued as he walked up and stood over the ruined man again and hissed, "And you know what I'll do if you let that happen? You know what I'll do? I will feed your entire family to your cursed, walking husk so that they don't have to live with the shame of your weakness."

Darius frowned, speechless. Even Vasna looked down and away, uncomfortable with the scene, and Andler's troops had slowed on the obstacle course, looking back at their brother-in-arms. They sped back into action when the general snapped his head back up, barking, "What are you slowing down for? Keep moving! This whimpering woman is dead! He's fertilizer!"

The prince, still cringing in disbelief, looked to Draad. "Can he do that?"

The high general shook his head. "As long as he doesn't lay a hand on his men, he's within the laws. I don't much like it either, but he isn't crossing the line."

Out on the field, the wounded soldier had begun to crawl toward a building that Darius assumed must be the infirmary. If he wasn't going to keep drilling, there was no reason to leave him to struggle. The prince took two steps in the direction of the man, but stopped short. Another general was almost there already.

The newcomer gestured to the crawling man. "This one not working out for you either, General?" He challenged Andler. "Strange how you keep getting the ones that aren't cut out for war. One might start to think they all have something in common."

"I don't know, Riggs," the menacing general barked back, stepping in to tower over the shorter one. "I haven't checked to see if they have any watered down coastlander blood running through their veins. Good thinking. I'll make a point to check."

Riggs was undaunted. "Back to the old standby then, I see. Well unless you have any legitimate criticisms, I'd like to take a look at your castoff here. See if I can't find a use for him."

Andler stepped even closer and growled something too

quietly for Darius to make out. It sounded like something about "prayers to pigeons," but that couldn't have been it. It didn't make any sense. Riggs, to his credit, still didn't flinch, but just narrowed his eyes. Darius listened harder now, managing to catch the shorter man's reply.

"You're not worth the effort, General." He held his ground for a moment more before he turned to attend to the soldier.

Riggs lifted the suffering man to his feet and got under his arm, supporting his weight and helping him to hobble off the field. He spoke quietly to the soldier, and though Darius couldn't hear his words, his expression was one not of coddling or babying, but of reassurance and encouragement. Whatever the general was saying seemed to be working. Some amount of color seemed to return to the soldier's face as he was passed off to the medics who had finally reached him at the drill yard's edge.

Darius murmured to himself, "So that's General Maxos Riggs."

Draad gave a proud grin. "Great tactician he is, and a good man too. The kind to lead by example, see?"

The prince kept watching General Riggs. Sure enough, the weathered leader returned to action and pushed through the obstacle course right alongside his men, keeping to the front of the pack and setting a pace to challenge his best. A few managed to beat Riggs through the course, and the general was the first to congratulate the men who did, clasping each man on the shoulder and encouraging his fellows to cheer for him.

Darius could only bite his lip. Of course it would play out like this. Regret crept into his heart for promising his father that he'd choose Andler to be his second. The prince glanced back at The Relentless. Its glory seemed to drain away, leaving it just a garish trophy he'd won at the price of his integrity. It loomed over him expectantly.

He sighed. He wouldn't break his word like the snakes he

hated. "High General, I need you to set up an appointment for me with General Andler later tonight. I have something to discuss with him."

Draad nodded. "Of course, Prince Vatri. There's a perfect meeting room in the command building. I'll have him meet you there as soon as drills are over." The high general bowed and strode away.

"You can't possibly be thinking of making that man an Aurora Knight," Vasna stated, as though it were fact and not question.

Darius narrowed his eyes at her. "What do you mean?" He hadn't mentioned to anyone except his father and a few of the shrine maidens that he'd had Watchward brought along.

"Prince Vatri," she explained bluntly, "if you think I don't have full knowledge of every single thing that enters and leaves my ship, you have underestimated me entirely."

The prince shook his head, setting aside his feigned ignorance. "You don't understand, Captain. I gave my word that I would select Andler. It's the only reason my father put you and The Relentless in my service."

"Well." She paused for a moment, wetting her lips with her tongue. "That was a very dumb thing to do. No reason to do a second dumb thing with me here to warn you against it."

Darius let her remark go unanswered, seeing as he felt like he'd earned her judgment, but went on resolutely as he began walking toward her ship to retrieve the legendary bow. "It doesn't work like that, Miss Hain. I gave my word. It's the one thing I still have at the end of the day that keeps all this royal blood from spoiling in my veins."

"I'm not sure I understand," she pressed him, before adding under her breath, "it's not a feeling I'm used to."

He sighed. "All I've ever wanted since I first heard stories of the great heroes of Vatrisland was to be one of them. Noble, honorable, self-made. Until my father got me this position, I was destined to sit at a throne and deal with bureaucrats. Now that I'm here, with a chance to be what I've wanted to be. I can't just turn my back on my honor."

She lengthened her strides to get in front of him and stepped in his way, bringing him to a stop. "Okay then." She took the tone of a scolding tutor. "Since you've given up entirely on operating under any logic or sense, I'll try to meet you halfway on this nebulous, touchy-feely territory you seem so fond of."

Darius' first instinct was to tell her exactly where to put her opinions on how he "operated," but some combination of curiosity and Vasna's naturally authoritative demeanor checked his urge. He crossed his arms and raised his eyebrows. "This I've gotta hear."

If he'd offended her, she didn't show it as she continued, "These heroes you're so enamored with? They couldn't always afford to do everything just so. Sometimes they had to make hard decisions to get the job done. They had to dirty their own names once in a while so others didn't have to suffer. And if you give one of the Aurora Arms to that man, he will tear apart any team you put together. No amount of honor is worth enduring him."

"Keeping your word when things start falling apart is hard, Captain. I don't like what I saw out there either, but what am I supposed to tell my father if I don't follow through on this? That I took the most sophisticated piece of magecraft in the kingdom's arsenal and then tossed my promise to the wind? I owe him this. I'd be soaking on the road and smelling of wet hound right now without his gift. I won't be so thankless."

She tucked her head and nodded, staying silent for a moment. "Okay, I see how it is."

"Thank you." He began again toward the ship.

"But one last thing."

Darius sighed, exasperated. "What?"

She didn't come around to face him this time, but stayed

where she was. "If you really aren't happy with what you're about to do, then consider this before you commit yourself to it," she offered. "Don't take the weapon to the meeting. Speak with Andler. Get to know him without letting him know what's on the line. If you still feel the same way at the end, all you've wasted is five minutes walking back to the ship to get it."

Darius considered her suggestion. What was five more minutes? A small enough price to pay to know General Andler as a person before he became a Knight, it seemed. He would have to be around Vasna for the foreseeable future, and there wasn't much hope she'd hold her tongue in the future if he didn't at least meet her halfway on something.

Darius turned around, intending to swiftly agree and be done with it, but for the briefest instant as he turned, he caught the expression Vasna had worn with no one looking. Her normally porcelain-smooth face was genuine and uneven. Human with concern for a fraction of a second before her perfect mask slipped back on.

"Okay," the prince said quietly. "Yeah, I'll do it."

She gave a single, sharp nod. "If you still feel the same afterward, you won't hear another word from me." She boarded The Relentless, adding, "And thank you, Prince Darius. You've made a very sensible decision."

9

Having seen no need to remain in his heavy armor into the evening, Darius had slipped into a shirt, vest, and comfortable trousers for his meeting with Andler. The prince now stood before the meeting room that the high general had indicated, ready to get to know his soon-to-be second-in-command. He pushed the door open to find the general wearing the calf-length crimson long coat of a Vatrisland officer's dress uniform, idly spinning a mounted globe with one hand, clutching a tall wooden mug with the other.

Andler slid the globe to a stop with his fingertips before turning to face Darius and bowing. "Prince Vatri, it is an honor to be in your presence, My Lord."

"At ease, General. I should have told Draad that I didn't need you in your formal attire to meet me. This is really more of a personal talk than official military business."

The general rose out of his bow, wrinkling his forehead in confusion. "I'm not sure I understand, My Lord. What would we be here to talk about if not military matters?"

Darius spun a hand in the air as he struggled to craft an explanation. It wasn't in his nature to mislead, but if he was going to get this untainted read of the man that Vasna had talked him into, he couldn't very well tell Andler the whole story. "I'm just trying to get a read on the officers out here. I'm expecting to go into battle beside you tomorrow, and I need to know who you are and how you think."

General Andler arched an eyebrow at the request for a

moment, but nodded nonetheless. "As you wish, My Lord." He picked up a second mug from a nearby table, offering it to the prince. "Care for a drink? We keep a cask of the best around for officers and honored guests."

Darius accepted the drink, thanking Andler as he did, and took a subtle sniff. Someone among the officers definitely knew his beer. "You've got quite a stout here, general. This is home away from home."

Andler grinned, wrinkling the jagged scar running down his cheek. "Worthy men should enjoy the privileges of their positions, mm? How about a toast then?"

"Please." Darius gestured with his mug, encouraging the general.

Andler raised his mug. "To Vatrisland! May the pure royal bloodline that has run through her kings for a thousand years run through your children and theirs for a thousand more, and may she reign supreme for all time."

"To Vatrisland," Darius agreed, though it seemed he hadn't done so emphatically enough for the general's tastes. He could feel Andler's eyes not just looking at him, but trying to burrow into him and figure him out as they drank.

He could see why his father had recommended the general. A few weeks ago Darius could have lifted his mug to it more sincerely, but now the conflicting expectations of his two positions stifled his enthusiasm. The toast made him wonder once more if he could really live with a foot in each of these two different worlds without tearing himself in half.

He finished the several long gulps he'd taken and seated himself at the table, motioning Andler to seat himself as well. "So, speaking of 'reigning supreme,' I'm told you're among the best we have. In an army like Vatrisland's, that's quite a boast."

Andler leaned back in his chair. "It's only boasting if it's an exaggeration, My Lord. I assure you it's not. Just look at my records. They're proof enough that I'm ready for a high generalship."

Darius could sense his irritation as he spoke. He took another sip from his mug before responding. "I take it you've applied for vacancies that have come up?"

"Three times now. Denied for each, if you must know."

Now Darius wished he'd looked at Andler's records like he had at Riggs'. There would have been detailed notes on why the reviewing officers had denied him. Even without those records, though, it was a red flag he didn't want to ignore.

But he'd promised.

"What did they say about why they'd denied you?" Darius asked.

The general rolled his eyes. "Said I lacked some kind of 'key leadership skills.' Just a polite way of saying that they prefer I stay their tool on the battlefield."

"You've got to admit that you handle your men differently than the other generals do, right?"

The general pursed his lips. "You're referring to the wounded soldier from the drills this afternoon."

No sense in skirting around the question then. Darius nodded. "I'll admit, I was taken off guard a bit by your approach."

Andler stood and looked straight at the prince, staring him down. "Was I wrong about what they'd do to him?"

Darius idly twisted his mug on the table. "No. No, I guess not."

The general went on, growing louder, "Then why should I treat these men like children, hm? Why should I tell them everything will be okay when it won't? I'm told to prepare them for the worst, but they chafe when I am not 'diplomatic' enough."

"Easy, General." Darius tried to calm him, but he'd clearly hit a raw nerve.

Andler shook his head, but he lowered his voice just

slightly. "Do you know how I got here, Prince Vatri? Do you know how this works? I'm a general today because I pressed on fighting monsters when I knew more of my men would die. I got the job done when others were afraid of the cost."

Darius narrowed his eyes. "Don't you think about the families these men leave behind?"

"That's exactly what I'm doing when I force them to fight on," the general hissed. "Make soldiers fight on, and soldiers die. Pull soldiers back, innocents die. Someone dies no matter what, Prince Vatri, and I get held back because I'm honest about it."

"These men aren't disposable, General."

"Aren't they?"

Silence fell over the room. The two men looked into each other's eyes, Darius questioning, Andler resolute.

The general gestured at Darius with mug in hand. "I know that look, My Lord. You'll have to forgive me if I seem unaffected by your judgment, but you cast it from a world of privilege. It's easy to keep one's hands clean if one never plays in the dirt."

Darius tightened his lips, resisting the urge to reprimand the general. He'd told Andler that it was a personal talk, so he couldn't fault the general for being candid. Even so, Vasna's plea for him to reconsider giving Andler Watchward was growing more and more wise.

But he'd promised.

The promise that he'd made to his father to choose Andler now stood in his gut like a wall, dividing his instincts from action. The very sense of honor that had defined him, even been his pride for so long, seemed suddenly like a puppeteer, manipulating him to satisfy its single-minded goal at any cost.

He needed to get away. He needed to think. "Maybe you're right, general. In any case, I appreciate your honesty," Darius said, rising from his seat. "Thank you for your time this evening. You've given me a lot to think about." The prince headed for the door.

"My Lord?" Andler spoke up once more, stopping him. "If I may give you one last thing to consider from my perspective. Vatrisland's army offers a total of twenty-three distinct medals and ribbons for valorous perseverance on the battlefield. I know. I've checked. I hold eight of them myself, two of which were even presented to me by your father with his blessing."

The general paused. Though Darius had his back turned, he heard the general step slightly closer before he continued. "There are no awards for retreat. This too I know, because I've checked."

Darius nodded once more, and headed out into the night without another word.

Night had fallen and Fort Diligence was quiet under the cloudless sky, save for the occasional chatter of patrolling sentries. Darius stepped out onto the central drill yard where he had watched Andler belittle the wounded soldier during the day. The ropes and nets that composed some of the obstacles swayed slightly in a dry, cooling breeze that slipped over the walls.

He had to come to a decision tonight if he wanted another Knight at his side for the journey into the Cryptwastes. There were too many unknowns beyond the barrier that had kept the Oracle from sensing the deepest reaches of the Cryptwastes to go in alone.

The Oracle. Darius slung the Titangavel's strap off of his shoulder and stared at it in his hands. He could call out to her through his weapon, but how would he explain the problem to her? To get her advice, he'd essentially have to confess to her that he'd accepted a bribe from Magnus. He tucked the hammer behind him once more, unable to bear the thought of bringing his shame to light. He'd have to resolve this on his own.

But even if he never explained his decision to the Oracle, Darius knew she'd lose all faith in him as soon as she knew he'd chosen Andler. On the other hand, to choose anyone else, he'd have to break his word to his father. No matter how he handled it, he'd have to betray somebody.

He could see why his father liked Andler. The general wasn't just a dedicated patriot, but also a man who would let the ends justify the means. He wouldn't waver if he had to make a decision that put other places or people at stake just to protect Vatrisland. The thought of coldly leaving innocents outside of his homeland to suffer disgusted Darius. It wouldn't be how the Aurora Knights worked if he had a say in the matter.

He climbed a staircase along the wall, and looked out on the southern horizon. Neither Cloudbreach nor the peaks of the Crown's Range were visible this far north, but the aurora was still faintly visible to the eye. It must have been truly vivid with magical power in the skies over the capital if Darius could see it from here tonight.

The more he thought on the matter, the more Andler really did seem a lot like his father. Both considered men tools to be used and discarded. Both took the straightest path to success without regard to who got hurt along the way. Neither gave a second thought to tearing a man down if he couldn't deliver a desired result. When the general behaved that way, Darius could muster disapproval, but when his father did the same, he was all too quick to concede.

The prince's face slowly wrinkled into a scowl. He'd prided himself on his ability to judge men evenly on their merits, but he'd let loyalty blind him to his father's hardheartedness. No man's position, whether familial or royal, should afford him a lower basic standard of decency.

That didn't justify Darius breaking his own word, though.

Did it?

Maybe he would have to. If he couldn't make himself recruit General Andler, and he couldn't break his word to his father, he was stuck at an impasse until he could decide which choice made him least offended with himself.

But he wasn't completely stuck. There was one thing he could still do. He took a deep breath to clear his thoughts and got directions to the personal quarters of General Maxos Riggs.

XXX

Though it had gotten quite late, Darius resolved himself to knock on General Riggs' door regardless. If he did decide to give Watchward to this general instead of Andler, it was probably better that Riggs know tonight. The alternative of meeting up with him the next morning with a hearty, "Nice to meet you! How would you like to be bound to a mystical artifact and charged with the world's safety?" seemed like it might be a lot to take in right before charging into battle.

Darius knocked on the general's door.

"Yes? Who is it?" came the muffled reply.

"This is Prince Darius Vatri. I need to speak with you, General."

"Of course, My Lord!" Darius could hear sounds of hurried footsteps from behind the door before it finally pulled open, revealing a sleepwear-clad General Maxos Riggs. He stood about two or three inches shorter than the prince, but what he lacked in height, he made up in lean muscle. A short, curly mop of light brown hair topped the general's tanned, weathered head. He looked as though he'd endured his share of rough experiences in his years with the army.

A faint scent of flowery incense wafted through the doorway as Riggs bowed to Darius. "My Lord, it's an honor."

"Relax, General," Darius reassured him. "Considering the hour, you have my apology."

"No, My Lord," the general replied, calming more as Darius had suggested. "I was just finishing something, so it's not a problem. Come in! I'll just need to put a thing or two away."

103

Riggs didn't wait for Darius to respond, and instead left the door open as he went to tidy his quarters. Darius regretted having to intrude on the man's personal space, especially considering that the general seemed eager to present himself at his best. There was a sincere and welcoming way about him though, to the point that the prince almost worried it might be an insult to refuse.

By the time Darius had cleared the doorway, Riggs had already rolled up a small mat and had tucked it under his bed. Dancing smoke caught the prince's eye and he followed it back to a shelf in a far corner of the room. A blue cylinder of pottery decorated with a series of small carvings held two sticks of smoldering incense. Crumbs of ash from the sticks dropped into a matching blue dish that fit snugly around the cylinder in the center. He searched his mind as he looked at the pieces. They seemed familiar somehow.

The general headed back over to the shelf, plucked the incense sticks from their sockets, and began to put away the arrangement, but Darius interrupted him. "General, what are those things? I feel like I've seen them before, but I can't place them."

Riggs stopped, suddenly uncertain and shy. "Oh, these," he started slowly, seeming to search for the right words. "Well, I...That is, my family rather. We pray to the Danma. My wife's H'tyanni. She got me started on it when we married."

The word snapped memories from Darius' schooling back to his mind. The Danma. He'd learned about them years ago from his tutors. Followers of the faith believed that this pantheon of fourteen spirits, each represented by a different iconic animal, created and governed everything throughout the world from physical things like weather and plants, to ideas like love or war.

Now the general's discomfort made perfect sense. Danmites were not looked upon favorably in Vatrisland. The faith had been founded long ago in the H'tyanni Empire and had never shaken the perception of being something foreign when it came to

104

his homeland. The closest thing his kingdom had to any sort of native faith was their reverence for the Aurora Knights, their Oracle, and the Arms, but that wasn't a faith so much as a respected tradition. The power that the Knights harnessed was an impersonal force, pulled from the mystical aurora and harnessed to accomplish things.

The Danmites, on the other hand, prayed in the morning and evening, and saw guidance in symbolism and happenstance. He'd watched his father explode in fury once when a profitable trade arrangement from the H'tyanni that had otherwise been coming together very well was abruptly withdrawn. When the foreign representative's pet frog died during negotiations, the entire H'tyanni delegation declared it a bad time to engage in trade. They packed up, left Cloudbreach, and refused to reconsider the offer until six months had passed.

The whole event had left King Magnus with an array of derogatory dead animal jokes prepared for any time something went bad between Vatrisland and the H'tyanni, regardless of whether Danmites were involved or not.

Darius reminded himself that the alternative to keeping an open mind with Riggs and his beliefs involved taking Watchward to Andler. He refocused his mind on the task at hand without pausing for too long. "Ah. How...How does it work?"

Riggs seemed to be a bit relieved at Darius' curiosity, and allowed him to take a closer look. "These are the fourteen spirits of the Danma," he explained, pointing to the icons. "There are seven for giving blessings along the top row, and seven for taking curses along the bottom. By each one, there's a spot to place incense. You only light it in front of the ones to whom you are praying at that time."

The prince looked over the array of intricately carved animals. The ones along the top had more docile or benevolent expressions. The bottom row were ferocious or sorrowful. "Mm.

105

And you only had two lit tonight?"

The general nodded, first pointing to a turtle along the top row, "Tonight, I prayed to Kashdi for her protection in tomorrow's battle."

"And the other?"

At that, Riggs looked less eager to explain, but still pointed to a hyena along the bottom, "To Grra," he explained, rolling the r sounds in the creature's name, "to take back his strife."

Darius narrowed his eyes in thought. "What happened to cause you strife?"

The general hesitated, biting his lip for a moment before offering, "My Lord, if you order me to explain, I will, but know that I would rather not."

Darius had been so intent on hiding his uncertainty with interest that he hadn't stopped to realize that he might be prying. "Of course, General. Forgive me."

"Thank you, My Lord." Riggs proceeded to empty the ashes from the dish piece and wrap each part in a cloth before stowing them in a small chest. Once finished, he offered Darius a chair and seated himself on his neatly made bed, seeming more at ease with the point of tension out of the way. "Now, how can I serve you?"

He had no better excuse now than he'd given Andler. Though Darius disliked being unable to reveal his actual motive for these meetings, he at least took comfort that his interest in getting to know the generals was genuine. "This isn't some kind of official meeting actually, so you don't have to be so formal. I just realized that tomorrow I'd be fighting alongside you and your men, so I wanted to know who you are and how you think. Those kinds of things," he explained.

Riggs clearly lit up at that. "I do the same with the men under my command. I find each one more willing and disciplined when I can call him by name, or remember what we talked about the last time we spoke off duty."

The prince grinned a bit. "So I noticed. I watched your crew drill for a little bit out there today. They seemed like they were all giving it their best. Saw you with that injured soldier from General Andler's group too, by the way."

Maxos took in a deep breath and sighed. "General Andler and I don't see eye-to-eye on many things. I couldn't stand by and watch that man suffer, under my command or not."

Darius already liked where this was going. He tried to play at being neutral to bait more out of the general. "I'm told that you and he have similar and impressive records. If he still gets results, what's wrong with his way?"

The general bit his lip, seeming to consider his next words carefully. "I could give you a number of explanations as a general, but you said that this wasn't an official inquiry of any kind. I take it you want to know what I think as a man, and not as a general, correct?"

Darius nodded.

"Then you need to know more about the Danma to understand," he went on. "I told you that we pray to ask for blessings to be given and for curses to be lifted, but there's more to it. The other part involves being the Danma for others, blessing and helping them when you can't find the way to what you're seeking. In this way, you invite blessing and help into your own life. So in hope of having my strife lifted, I lift strife from the lives of others."

"Hm," Darius grunted. The whole system seemed strange to him. Who was to say that the Danma had anything to do with all of this blessing and recovering? Seemed like the kind of thing that could easily be chalked up to coincidence, or at least the likelihood that if you went around being good to enough people, you were bound to meet someone who could help you solve your problems.

"Well, if nothing else, you'll have plenty of strife to lift as long as you're deployed in the same place as Andler," he said, hoping he didn't sound too skeptical of Maxos' faith.

The brief, uncomfortable silence that followed made it clear that he'd failed.

"Look," Maxos finally offered, "I don't hope to see sudden conversions or things like that when I talk about my faith. I've been married for six years now, and have followed this for five. I've endured scorn from my friends in back home for praying to 'foreign ghost animals,' and I've lost touch with others over it entirely."

He stood up to continue, but even as he approached his point, he still spoke gently. "But if the ends can justify the means for Andler with all of his temper and venom, why not for me too? No one should care that the idea that makes me a better general comes from outside of the borders of Vatrisland, and yet here we are, casting it into question."

Darius' heart sunk. Maxos was right. Vatrisland's rulers, commanders, and even many of the common people would gladly accept a ruthless patriot over a man of genuine virtue like Riggs with foreign influences guiding him. Why should he care where the general's goodwill and sincerity came from? What was most important was that he could depend on the general to act for good under pressure. How had he been ready to second guess the man's potential over something ultimately insignificant?

"General, I didn't mean to offend," he said, standing as well. "You're right. It doesn't make a damn bit of sense that we judge you more harshly than we judge Andler. It seems like we— rather, I—have some curses of my own that could use lifting."

Maxos seemed taken off-guard by his apology, his mouth left hanging open for a few moments before he found his words. "My Lord, I'm not sure what to say. Coming from you, that kind of humility means a lot. I've got to say I didn't expect the Prince of Vatrisland to be this openminded." The general paused, looking down before he continued. "It's no wonder you were chosen to be the Captain of the Aurora Knights. When I first heard, I'd had my doubts that someone in your position could take on the role without bias, but it's clear that the Oracle made the right decision."

Darius froze. That's right. Nobody aside from himself, his father, and the Oracle knew the conditions under which he'd been made the leader of the Knights. No one else knew that his father had pulled the strings, and that out there somewhere was the man who had been intended for the position. Did that hero even know that his position had been usurped? Would he be told why it had happened? Or would he, like Riggs did now, believe that the Darius had been the candidate all along?

He shook his head and set those thoughts aside. He couldn't afford to stay fixated on the past. The Oracle had made plans for a different person to lead the Knights, but when she'd been forced to adapt at his father's insistence, she had done what she had to do to protect the world. She hadn't refused to act when things started falling apart. She'd played the hand she'd been dealt, and done her best to support him and put her hopes in him.

Now Riggs was putting his hopes in Darius too. The general believed in him, and trusted him to make the right decisions even though he hadn't fit the mold Riggs had imagined. That shrine maiden, Charise, had also been uncomfortable with how he'd behaved, and yet she'd soldiered on and tried her best in spite of it.

Everyone was making sacrifices to adapt for his sake.

He'd made his father a promise.

But he couldn't let that stand in the way of doing what was clearly, unquestionably right.

"General Riggs, put some shoes on. I need to show you something out by The Relentless."

Maxos cocked his head at the prince, but obeyed. Together, the two walked out to the ship, and Darius went inside briefly to retrieve Watchward. He came back out with the bow wrapped in a cloth, and addressed the general there before the ramp that extended from the ship.

"General Maxos Riggs, your record of service already proves that you're a capable fighter and a competent leader. But beyond that, tonight you've proven to me that you're wise and decent too. You've given me perspective on my shortcomings, and shown me that you have the will to press on in the face of challenges when you know you're doing what's right."

"My Lord, I—" Riggs began.

Darius cut him off. "I can think of no one I'd rather have at my side in battle carrying Watchward, General. Fight beside me. Become an Aurora Knight."

Riggs struggled to speak as Darius unfolded the cloth wrapping the weapon. In the light of the moon, the pale, supple wood of Watchward seemed to almost glitter. Swirling designs of wind and storm cradled an eye-shaped emerald set just above the grip. Unlike the hulking Titangavel, Watchward rested so lightly in Darius' open arms that he had to look at it to know for certain it was still there.

"This," Maxos began, "is not what I expected."

"Is that a 'no'?"

"No! Not at all! It's just...." He seemed to search for the right words. "...A strange answer to my prayers, let's say."

Darius arched an eyebrow at that. "Can I take that to mean you accept?"

The general considered it for a moment more before he nodded resolutely. "Yes, My Lord. I accept."

The men smiled. Neither spoke for a moment until Maxos added, "So, is there some kind of ceremony? Do we need a witness? Or do I just pick this up and that's that?"

"Well, you've got your witness."

The two looked behind Darius. Vasna Hain stood at the top

of the ramp dressed in a black, loose fitting top and pants that wavered slightly in the breeze. She leaned against the frame of the hatch with her arms crossed, smirking.

The prince returned her expression. "I didn't see anyone up and about when I went in. Figured you were asleep."

"Did you think I was kidding when I told you I was aware of every single thing that entered and left my ship?" she asked, playfully offended. "Do I look prone to exaggeration?"

Darius shook his head and looked back at Maxos. The Oracle had passed onto him the rite by which to Knight his chosen allies when the time came, and he spoke it now from memory.

"Maxos Riggs, as the Knight-Captain of the Aurora Knights, I hereby bind to you Watchward, the Vigilant. Take up this weapon and defend the world in the face of its most desperate hour. As of this day, you are an Aurora Knight."

10

"Stars, Oracle. That's a lot of undead."

Darius stood on the deck of The Relentless, clad once again in his full armor and gripping the railing as he peered over the side at the expanse of the Cryptwastes far below. Beside him, Maxos watched as well, clad in lighter layers of chain and leather. In the distance, countless undead formed a battlefront at least a mile long and nearly half that deep. Pale forms clad in rusty armor made up the front most ranks, but he could pick out clusters of other figures giving off a sickly, violet glow that unnerved him. Larger reanimated warbeasts, once buried with the rulers whom they served, plodded along with the legions, towering taller than full-grown elephants as they shook their massive horned heads side-to-side.

Her voice echoed back into the prince's head. "I can see them on our map here. They've passed through the veil that kept me from scrying on them while I slept. It's definitely a larger force than Vatrisland's intelligence previously indicated."

Maxos nodded, also speaking to the Oracle, "The scouts tracking this group said that it's been further reinforced in the past twelve hours." He offered Darius a grim frown. "Perhaps their leader heard that we've brought out the Arms, My Lord."

"Maybe," Darius replied, turning from the railing to face him. "And hey, I told you to knock off that 'My Lord' stuff. You're an Aurora Knight now, Maxos."

"Sorry, My," Maxos stopped and corrected himself.

"Darius. You're still Prince of Vatrisland."

The prince chuckled. "I've lived in a sea of titles all of my life, Maxos. They're suffocating if you ask me. As long as we're both Aurora Knights, we're brothers in arms."

Maxos looked back over the railing, "Well Darius, ready to set the example for the men of our homeland?" he asked, gesturing as the skyship banked, bringing their own forces into view.

Darius sized up their group against the undead. They were clearly outnumbered, maybe by as much as two to one, and against a foe that didn't know panic or pain. Still, even five hours into the day, the troops of Vatrisland kept order as they marched forward. Most of them were foot soldiers with spellblades, but they were well supported by a number of specialist units too. Mounted riders clad in the heaviest armor sat atop loyal and eager riding hounds armored in heavy barding. A rare and valuable unit of warmages brought up the rear. Vatrisland treated the few mages skilled enough to cast their powerful, explosive spells very well, even going as far as assigning them their own personal bodyguards for battle. Though the assault would exhaust them quickly, their well-placed blasts of power could take out crowds of foes at a time. The nation didn't risk losing power like that to a stray arrow or assassin's blade.

And on top of all of that, Vatrisland's forces would be accompanied by two Aurora Knights. Darius turned his head to hide a grin from Maxos, suspecting that the older man wouldn't understand his thrill. This was it. Darius' first real battle lay ahead of him. Today, he'd finally have the chance to begin building his own heroic legend, destined to go down in Vatrisland's history. He imagined the victory parade, and the statue of him they would erect near the castle. The masons wouldn't be chipping out his form clad in kingly robes, but in shining armor with the Titangavel at his side. Just the thought of his future monument left him giddy.

The Oracle snapped him back into the moment again.

"Have no doubt that you're both ready for this. These are exactly the kind of challenges that the Aurora Arms equip you to handle."

"Of course we're ready. I was born ready! Come, Maxos!" he shouted, hoping he could pass off his boyish enthusiasm for the fight as confident resolve. "Let's join them on the ground. It won't be long now."

The two headed onto the bridge from the windy top deck, and Darius called out, "Captain Hain, bring us down to land! Maxos and I will be joining up with the troops."

"Over my dead body."

Darius looked at the captain and cocked his head to one side. She sure looked pretty appalled for such a simple request as she clicked her boots across the bridge toward him. He managed to catch Pierce and Treve trading smirks before she came to a stop right in front of him.

"If you think I'm going to put the most expensive, most complex piece of magecraft I've ever designed to ground in an uncontrolled environment with an army of undead and a powerful necromancer within spitting distance," she stated, crossing her arms defiantly, "you're about to be entirely disappointed."

Maxos raised one eyebrow. "How do you see us disembarking then, Captain?"

She paused, pursed her lips as she thought, and declared, "I'll have a rope ladder lowered from the deck. You can climb down and I'll be able to maintain a fifteen foot ground clearance."

"Or we could jump," Darius offered.

Maxos and Vasna cocked their heads at him.

"Might be pretty impressive," he continued, managing to keep an even tone to cover his excitement. "I've dropped from over three stories with the Titangavel at my side. Barely felt it."

"I don't know that undead get impressed," Maxos countered, clearly skeptical.

"No, but men do. Our forces haven't seen the Aurora

Knights in action yet. The last group of Knights served before any of us were born. A good show of our power could boost their confidence."

"Brilliant. Love it," Vasna quipped flatly. "I'm getting inspired just thinking about it."

Darius shook his head, chuckling. "Come on, Maxos. We'll have them pop the hatch down below." The two wove their way through the corridors of the ship to their usual exit.

Once they arrived at the lower hatch, it took a few moments to convince a crewman that they were serious, but eventually the man strapped on goggles and tethered himself to a pipe near the hatch control. Darius could tell that his excitement was contagious. Though the man had been reluctant at first, by the time he was preparing to actually pull the lever, he too was grinning eagerly.

The Knights found fixtures to grip as well when the hatch began to open. Darius felt a wild rush as he looked down onto the Cryptwastes from this new perspective with no waist-high railing to reassure him. Though he knew the powers of the Aurora Arms would carry him to land safely, his instincts had not yet adjusted to his new capabilities. As wind whipped through the open hatch, his heartbeat pounded in his ears and temples.

Maxos gave him an "after you" gesture. The prince nodded and, with a running start, barreled out into the open air, Titangavel in hand, streaking toward the ground.

He squinted down at the army. Though it was tough to make out details clearly, he could see portions of the group halting. No doubt they'd been startled to see two small objects streaking out of the sky toward them. With all the attention, Darius couldn't resist the urge to make his entrance even showier. He thrust his arms out from his sides and spiraled, letting out a loud, ecstatic whoop as he did.

"Did I give that weapon to a boy, or to a man?" the Oracle's disapproving voice questioned in his head.

Darius retorted, his laughter drowned out lashing gusts. "No appreciation for the value of showmanship, Oracle? The men down there are going to love—"

Suddenly, a blinding flash of light and heat shot past him, leaving a crash of thunder in its wake. Fighting disorientation, he pulled out of his spiral and brought his feet out in front of him. Not a moment later, he landed in a crouch with a resounding crash, cratering the ground as he did.

Vatrisland's troops erupted into loud cheers as he stood to his full height. Darius looked around to see where the flash had come from, only to see Maxos standing a nearby on a smoking scorch mark. "Power of lightning," the general murmured. Maxos' twirled Watchward in his hands, his look of surprise giving way to a thrilled smile.

"You sure picked up how to use your powers quickly," Darius remarked, plainly impressed.

For a split second, Maxos seemed to hesitate. Not a moment after Darius noticed it, the general just shook his head. "It's nothing. You spend enough time on the battlefield, and you'll learn how to adapt to new things this quickly too."

Darius smirked. Perhaps Maxos was a deeper well than he'd initially thought. Or maybe the Aurora Arms just had a way of making a guy push his limits. He had to admit, it was hard to show restraint knowing he had all of that power at his fingertips.

Eager to not be outdone, the prince thrust the Titangavel upward, raising a small stage of pale, cracked earth beneath himself so the men further back could see him as well. From there, the sea of soldiers that had looked like ants from far above now looked mighty, ordered, and battle-ready. They quieted as he sought their attention.

"Soldiers of Vatrisland, today we break this stalemate," Darius shouted to them. Even his voice seemed stronger with his weapon at his side, and he could see men far to the back of the crowd thrusting their fists skyward in agreement. "I know many of you have been stationed out here for months now. You're eager to get home, to see your families and your friends."

He turned sideways to them, pointing the Titangavel out at the undead army in the distance. "Well, somewhere out among those dusty shamblers is the ticket home. There's a necromancer keeping charge over all of them, and if we take him out, these things will lose the mind that keeps them all in order."

Maxos leapt up beside him at that and added to the speech. "But this foe will be powerful. If you find him, give him a wide berth and point us toward him. Darius and I will do our best to defeat him quickly, but we cannot be everywhere at once, so remember the training and the discipline that have made you the world's finest army."

The troops burst into loud cheers again. Darius looked to Maxos and nodded. He never would have thought to put all of their eyes to work finding the leader. The general just kept further proving he was the right man to carry Watchward, and if he fought as well as he led, Darius doubted he'd have any trouble justifying his decision to his father when he finally came clean about going back on his word.

The prince turned his eyes to the army once more, and judging them to be more than adequately motivated, directed his platform to lower with the Titangavel.

"Prince Vatri!"

Darius followed the voice to see General Andler emerging from the crowd. He avoided eye contact as he approached. "Yes, General," the prince began.

Andler replied quietly, still not meeting his gaze. "I could not help but notice that you arrived without a second-in-command, My Prince, and now you stand before us beside General Riggs."

Darius bit his lower lip, nodding, hoping the hot-tempered officer didn't aim to make a scene right now. "That's correct."

"I am not a fool, Prince Vatri," Andler went on. "I know now that our conversation before was not what it seemed. I also know that there are three more Aurora Arms that I have not yet seen out here, and I cannot think of any reason for you to hide their bearers if they have been chosen already."

The general then looked him in the eye. Darius had hoped that perhaps he'd see the man apologetic for how he behaved with the soldiers under his command, but Andler's expression was wholly one of frustration. "Consider me, then, for one of the remaining weapons, Prince Vatri. You know me to be a true patriot and a fearsome fighter. Let me assure your victory. Let me fight at your side."

Darius contained his disappointment. Andler had no idea what he was doing wrong, there was no time to explain. Still, even as disappointed as he was, he couldn't simply tell Andler "never." Darius knew that the last few days alone had changed how he himself now behaved and thought. Noting that, he couldn't leave the general completely without hope.

"General, focus on today's battle. I promise I will continue to watch you and consider what you've asked, but for now, keep your mind in the moment."

The general saluted. "Yes, Prince Vatri. Thank you." He turned away from the prince and made his way back into the crowd.

A call from Maxos brought Darius back to attention. "They're almost upon us! Ready yourselves!" At that, the prince hustled over to Maxos' side. Behind him, the chorus of swords being drawn from thousands of sheaths sang out. Across the expanse, the shuffling horde accelerated, each desiccated skeleton and necrotic horror moving with its own unique, unnatural gait dependent on which parts of its frame and limbs were still intact. The great preserved warbeasts surged forward too, adding their ominous rumbling footfalls to the chaotic array of noises.

"Darius?"

The Oracle's voice cut through the noise of the approaching enemies easily. He'd intended to get a final word from her before the battle began, but now was cutting it a bit close. "Yeah, yeah," he spoke quickly. "We're just about to get into the thick of it."

"Really? From here it appears that they're charging at you."

Darius looked out at the horde. "And that's why we're about to get into the thick of it."

Apparently, the communication that his weapon allowed even extended to Ria's annoyed sigh. "I should have contacted you again myself," she said. "Well, know that we are here for you back at Aurora Tower. Tell us whatever you can as you fight. My maidens are ready to research any details you can provide."

"Got it. Wish me luck, Oracle," Darius answered. He had to admit, it comforted him to know that the maidens were working to support him back at the castle.

"Warmages, ready," came the shout from the back ranks. Even over the din of the undead charge, Darius heard the tinkle and hum of coalescing magics reach its crescendo. At the signal to fire, motes of shining, concentrated power streaked across the skies overhead, leaving a piercing whistle in their wake. They sped like bolts of lightning into the horde, exploding on impact with bright, colorful flashes, casting bones and dust in all directions.

"Kashdi defend us," Maxos murmured under his breath. "They never slow down."

It was true. Men might have scattered, or at least flinched charging into the magical assault that had just leveled dozens of their number. The Vatrislanders wouldn't be able to count on such an advantage here. The relentless mass didn't even slow, and more skeletal forms raced forward to fill the gaps left by those destroyed.

Maxos clasped Darius on the shoulder for a moment as the

warmage commander signaled to ready a second volley. "This'll be it. They'll cut to more precise spells after this volley so they don't hit us. Ready?"

Darius nodded, readjusting his grip on Titangavel. There would be nobody to dismiss those great warbeasts if he were crushed today like he had been by the conjured jinra in training. All the excitement that he'd enjoyed in the past few days suddenly felt a little childish as he stood before the grim, rampaging force. The challenge and stakes became real, made concrete before him in the eyeless gazes his enemies.

Another volley of explosive magic raced overhead, striking true once again to leave more shallow, scorched craters where enemies had stood a moment before.

The order to charge rang out.

Darius only heard the rising drumming of footfalls behind him for a moment before he and Maxos sprinted ahead. Not even the houndsmen with their mounts spurred to charge could keep pace with the two Knights powered by their Arms.

Maxos took advantage of Watchward's powers as they closed the distance, drawing back on its bowstring. A white, crackling needle of lightning formed where he gripped before fanning into five as he spread his fingers on the taut weapon. Even at a full sprint, the general's aim was faultless, and every shot in the volley struck its target squarely in the chest, splintering bone with resounding thunderclaps.

Darius had no intention of being outdone. He bounded into the air, drawing back the Titangavel over his head with a loud war cry. He came down on his target with an explosive slam, sending a wake of earthy spikes lancing out in a wave ahead of him. The horde closed in around him, but their numbers meant little as he lashed out with the hammer from side to side, crushing three or four of them with each swing.

Behind the Knights, the soldiers of Vatrisland crashed into

the front lines of the undead army and set to work with their flashing spellblades. Darius caught sight of the houndsmen seated high on their mounts lashing out with their weapons, too. Their dogs snarled and snapped, snatching unwary skeletons by their hips or ribs and shaking them to pieces.

A flash of lightning ripped through the undead crowd and broke into the clearing Darius had begun to make with the wide, arcing swings of the Titangavel. The light faded to reveal Maxos, who stepped into position back-to-back with Darius and continued unleashing volleys from Watchward.

"How are we doing?" Darius called out over the cries and clattering weapons. He'd been told that huge battles like this would be chaotic and confusing, but his imagination hadn't done it justice.

"We're holding from the look of things," Maxos shouted back. "But it's too soon to...." The general trailed off.

"Too soon to what?" Darius prompted, pulverizing another bony soldier that had dared to test him.

"Well, now we know what we saw glowing out here."

"Let me see!" At Darius' request, the two spun, keeping their backs pressed together so that the prince could see out into the sea of undead again. Just beyond the skeletal forces before him, he could see that same, unsettling light that he'd spotted from the deck of The Relentless.

Then they emerged. A cluster of mummified corpses shambled forward, their wrappings scribed with runes emitting a sorcerous violet glow. They hunched under the weight of gold and jewels that they had proudly worn in life as they approached. Their desiccated lips peeked out from beneath the strips wrapping their faces, now shrunken too much to close over clenched teeth.

Nearby, soldiers began to back away from their new foes as terror gripped them. Many even left openings in their panic and were cut down. Darius gritted his teeth and held his ground. He felt the same fear, but if he fled, the men behind him would run as well. The burden of setting an example was just one more surprise lesson he hadn't expected to learn today.

Steeling his will with a roar, the prince lashed out with the Titangavel at the nearest mummy, but they were quicker than their hunched forms let on. It ducked his swing and rose to its full height again inside his arms' reach, gripping his forearm as it did.

The cold pain that shot through the prince's arm seared like nothing he'd felt before. A choked cry escaped his throat as he saw the creature's touch crumble his armor as though it had been made of dry bread. He struggled to break free of the hand now tightly gripped on his arm, but his muscles barely offered any force now. The creature let out an unearthly, sucking wail, nearly nose-to-nose with him.

"Darius!" Maxos whipped around into a crouch and fired a full spread of five bolts into the horror at point-blank range. They caught it in the chest, lifting it into the air and ripping its body free of its grappling hand. Darius toppled, grunting at the throbbing pain that left his ears ringing, and pried the severed limb loose from his arm. The skin that the mummy had gripped had withered and blackened, and all muscles beyond his shoulder refused to do anything other than tremble.

"Get—" Maxos began, but every time he tried to speak, another foe closed forcing him to whirl around for another shot. He finally gripped Darius' armor where some of the plates had separated and sprang into the air with a sloppy, off-balance leap. The two hurtled over the battle out of control, somehow managing to land back among their own troops without colliding with anyone. Darius hit the ground flat on his back, forcing the wind out of his lungs, leaving him gasping.

"Are you okay, My Lord?" Maxos asked, whipping his head back and forth between Darius and the oncoming enemy.

Darius didn't answer. He braced himself on his good arm

and looked into the fray. Without the power of the Aurora Arms, the soldiers were no match for these new abominations. He watched, helpless, as one lifted a man off the ground by the throat one-handed and withered him. The soldier barely had time to scream before he was reduced to a dried, blackened husk.

He was failing them. He and Maxos were the only ones who could stand against these, and he was lying on the ground whimpering. Darius looked down at his injured arm. His powers were doing their job. The withered blotch was regaining color, and his hands, though now without armor to cover them, were back under his control. "I told you n-not to call me that," he scolded Maxos as the pain started to subside.

The general nodded. He turned and flashed back into lightning, bull rushing into the nearest foe with a thunderclap.

Darius shook the last of the trembles off, pulling himself to his feet. He had to get back into the battle. If normal men couldn't weather a strike from these creatures, he had to put down as many as he could so they could handle the skeletons.

"Prince Vatri!"

Darius looked for the source of the call. A moment later, a short, pale soldier slipped out of the crowd and into view. Blood trickled from a gash on his forehead, and he collapsed to his knees looking dizzy and winded.

"What is it, soldier?"

"We've found the necromancer, My Lord," the soldier continued between hastily gulped breaths. "General Andler and his men have engaged him! He's atop one of the beasts. I came to tell you like General Riggs ordered!"

Darius swore. Andler was going to get himself killed trying to prove his worth. "Which way?" he barked at the soldier. Once the man had pointed him in the right direction, the prince ordered him to back up, and commanded the ground beneath his own feet to rise using the Titangavel.

123

He scanned the battlefield quickly, not daring to stay elevated so high for too long. It was difficult to make any sense of the chaotic sea of metal, flesh, dust, and bone, but he still squinted in the direction the soldier had indicated. Sure enough, he managed to pick out one of the massive, undead beasts with a small, black shape riding atop it.

Darius lowered himself back into the crowd, swearing under his breath. He looked at Maxos and called out to him through the Titangavel. "Maxos, I can see the Necromancer! I'm going to take him out! Stay here and see if you can keep those things off of our men!"

Maxos' voice came back, "Darius, wait! Don't try it alone! We'll hit him together!"

The prince made no reply. He set out bounding across the battlefield toward the necromancer.

11

With the battle in the Cryptwastes in full swing, the top chambers of Aurora Tower became a bustling war room to support the Aurora Knights. Ria oversaw the table in the center of the vault, shifting its illusory projection back and forth to view Darius or Maxos as she needed. She spoke through Watchward with Maxos, prodding him to give more and more detailed descriptions of the mummified sorcerers that sapped the lives of Vatrisland's soldiers. A team of shrine maidens buzzed about the room hard at work too. Some paged rapidly through books, looking for symbols and patterns that Maxos reported on the creatures he fought. Others stayed in communication with The Relentless or Fort Diligence as needed via the magic mirrors, funneling in the information that Vasna and her crew gathered from their unique perspective above the fight.

The terse voice of Maxos Riggs echoed through the Oracle's head. "I can't give you a better description, Oracle! I'm"—the general paused to give a grunt of exertion—"multitasking!"

"General, we need more." Ria kept her voice calm and clear in spite of her mounting frustration. She longed for the transcendent state of her meditative sleep that she'd come to take for granted over the years. In it, she could have easily seen the exact symbols and pictographs on the creatures and relayed them to her maidens. Instead, she struggled to make crude sketches and notes on a stray piece of parchment. "Look harder at their amulets.

You said you saw a creature of some kind depicted on them. I need to know what it was."

"As soon as I can!" he barked.

She paused to let him work, taking a moment to look at the bright side. At least she could count Maxos among the Knights at all. Though it would be a struggle to keep the news that Darius had gone back on his word to his father, she'd made sure that the news had been spread among all of the shrine maidens. They'd all been warned to just refer to Riggs as "the general" at all times to keep the truth under wraps. As far as she knew, none of them had been put to the test yet, but she trusted her maidens to stay mindful of their plan.

Ria waved her hand over the table to refocus it on Darius and the Titangavel. The prince was still making his way across the battlefield, bounding back and forth between the enemy force and his own and occasionally striking rumbling blows, thinning the densest clusters of undead.

"Darius, be careful as you approach this necromancer," Ria warned sternly. "If he can hold an army of this size under his control, there's no telling what else he's capable of."

"I've got my eyes open, Oracle. I'm almost to him. It's strange—"

"What's strange?" Ria interrupted quickly. In hindsight, she realized that her chiming in would only slow down his explanation, but she couldn't help herself. Strange was bad. Strange meant they lacked the full picture about something going on.

"Andler and some of his men have made it far enough to engage this guy," he shouted through their link. "Seems like he's only defending himself though! He's not killing any of them, he's just deflecting their attacks!"

Ria pondered it. That really was strange. Even novice necromancers learn to sap life with their powers long before they learn to control undead. Furthermore, why wouldn't a necromancer want to kill more of Vatrisland's troops? Once they were dead, he could raise them to bolster his army. It would be a win-win situation for him.

She wasn't given time to speculate further on it. The loud tapping of shoes interrupted her as Charise dashed across the antechamber and up into the vault where Ria stood. She panted and gulped in breaths. "The king! H-he's coming up here. We tried to s-stop him but he's having his guards escort him in!"

Ria set aside her speculations on the necromancer and refocused on her new crisis. "Everyone!" she shouted, clapping her hands over her head to get their attention. "Everyone, remember what I told you earlier. It is absolutely critical that King Magnus not know who carries Watchward. Do as you were prepared to and behave naturally. You can do this."

Each of the women called back a reply of, "yes Oracle," as she could break concentration on her own task. No more than they'd finished responding, the large, elevating disc just beyond the antechamber hummed to a stop. King Magnus strode in, accompanied by four armed guards.

"Oracle, it troubles me that I would have to be accompanied by guards to come see you," he growled. "Have your maidens forgotten whose castle grounds their tower stands upon, or should I have greater cause to take offense?"

Ria put all of her effort into concocting the right mix of apology and irritation for her response. "I'm sorry, your majesty, but the Knights are in battle alongside your troops, and I feared your presence would inadvertently distract my maidens." Ria glanced about the room. Several of the maidens were looking over their shoulders nervously instead of working. "Which, as you can see, it has!" she scolded.

The women snapped back to task, some with their hands quivering slightly.

King Magnus stepped up from the antechamber into the vault room with his guards trailing behind him. "Perhaps you should reconsider your perspective on the issue. Vatrisland's troops are fighting and dying out there too. Shouldn't her king have every right to be informed about the conflict killing his own men?"

She couldn't very well resist further without drawing more suspicion. "Of course, your majesty. Make yourself comfortable. I will personally answer any questions you have as best I can."

"That's more like it. I knew we could reach an understanding, Oracle." Magnus directed his guards off to stand against the walls nearby and began to observe the illusory map and the tiny forces waging war on it.

"Oracle! I got a better look! It's like a cobra head!" Maxos' shout rang through Ria's head.

"Excellent work, General," Ria replied before turning to her researching maidens, "Narrow your search, ladies! Cobra iconography! Get me something I can work with!" The team at the research table quickly sorted books into two piles before sweeping one off of the table onto a nearby cart.

"That's right, isn't it?" The king chimed in. "You can speak with them through their weapons. How is General Andler working out for you? No doubt he's killed more than my boy, considering his experience."

The Oracle replied naturally and evenly. "The General is doing an excellent job, your majesty. He's proving to be of great help to your son." Though she felt she had been convincing, she needed him to change the subject to Darius. On that, at least she wouldn't have to so actively screen her every word.

He seemed to take her prompt. "Mm. And how is Darius doing?"

"I've fixed our view on him and the Titangavel. You can see for yourself," she said, drawing his attention further onto the red mote of light that highlighted Darius' position. She could feel the tension in the room lifting as they got further from the subject of Maxos.

"Oracle," came Darius' voice in her head next. "Oracle! I think he saw me! They're routing!"

Ria's attention snapped to the rear of the undead army at the very edge of her view out from Darius' position. Sure enough, the furthest forces were receding back into the Cryptwastes, and the army was shifting to pursue. That didn't make sense, though. The undead force still looked far larger than Vatrisland's. "Darius, I don't like this," she warned him. "Be very careful. Turn back if something doesn't look right."

"I can't just let this guy get away…acle! We can…nd this to…ay."

Sudden confusion and panic gripped Ria. Darius' voice was fading in and out. This was not the kind of thing that happened haphazardly. Something was interrupting their connection. She swept her hand over the terrain on the table, but now the undead horde and the ruby red blip that represented Darius had faded from sight. Even more disturbing was the sight of Vatrisland's troops vanishing from the map in a crisp, distinct line as they crossed some invisible threshold.

Magnus could see the Oracle's growing fear and seized on it with judgment. "Oracle, what is wrong? Why are my men disappearing?"

She didn't have time to entertain his question. "General? General!" She cried out, but the far end of the army where Maxos had been was slipping beyond her reach too. Her effort to recenter the map on him only left her spotting a faint, emerald sparkle just dying out. She struggled to stay focused and think of her next step, but the sudden and absolute unknown had disarmed her.

"Oracle! Answer me! What is going on?" The king refused to relent.

"I don't know," was all she could muster. The stunned maidens near her looked around in panic as well, struggling to find something, anything that might point them toward the next step.

Charise's voice rose out of the chaos, shouting in what was the loudest display Ria had ever heard from her. "Oracle! The Relentless! It's still there!"

Ria looked to her map. The Relentless hadn't crossed the line yet, and was only drifting slowly toward it. Ria rushed over to one of the magical mirrors on the wall and put her hand to its frame, concentrating on her memory of the skyship's bridge. "Captain Hain! Captain, are you there? Stop your ship! Stop!"

The ship's bridge faded into view along with the stern, commanding presence of Vasna Hain. "You heard her! Stop, Pierce! Full-stop!"

The Oracle couldn't help but look back across the room at the glowing map on the table. The tiny image of The Relentless halted itself a safe distance from the edge where the troops had vanished.

Ria nearly collapsed in relief, thankful for some connection to the battle that she could still hold onto. Vasna looked back at her from the mirror. "We're stopped, Oracle. What's wrong?"

"Captain, what happened to the army? What happened to my Knights?"

"What do you mean? They're still straight ahead. They're chasing that blighter and his minions into the hills!" the captain answered.

"They're still there?" Ria pondered aloud. Nothing was suddenly consuming them, but something was hiding them from her. She hadn't felt this helpless since—

Her eyes widened. It was the field she'd felt in her sleep! It had to be the same veil that had kept her from looking into the Cryptwastes as she had scryed. "Captain, something is keeping me from contacting the Knights. I need you to get ahead of them and

130

warn them to fall back! The retreat is a feint. They're cutting Vatrisland's entire force off from us. That monster is up to something."

Vasna nodded to the Oracle and looked away to command her crew, "Pierce! Get ahead of our men!" The captain braced for a moment as The Relentless lurched into motion. "Don't worry, Oracle. Darius and Maxos are fast, but they can't outpace this ship."

"Did you just say 'Maxos'?"

Ria froze as her receding dread surged back through her at the sound of Magnus' voice. The shrine maidens had quieted too. The only sounds were the hum of The Relentless surging forward and the soft footfalls of the king as he stepped into Vasna's view.

Magnus spoke again, sounding eerily calm. "Captain Hain, who is my son's second-in-command?"

Not even Vasna's signature, unflappable cool could keep her jaw from going slack as she realized what she'd just done.

"Captain, answer me."

Vasna didn't get time to reply. She swore as the ship rocked hard to one side with a loud bang, lifting her off of her feet and tossing her out of sight. A blinding flash shined out of the mirror. It faded, leaving only the reflections of the stunned Ria and narrow-eyed Magnus behind her.

The Oracle spun to face the king, wide-eyed.

"Oracle," he stated, looking into her eyes with absolute coldness, "I am not pleased."

A flickering light behind Magnus caught Ria's eye. It emanated from the map upon the table, where half of the illusory terrain had been replaced with an arc of quivering light. Beyond it, the table stood bare.

12

The loud blast and crackle coming from behind Darius was his first indication that something was wrong. He looked back to see The Relentless approaching fast and coming in low. A sizable crack in one of the huge crystals that propelled it spat uncontrolled arcs of magical energy.

The skyship was crashing.

"Maxos! The Relentless!" he called out to his friend as the vessel sailed over his head and the teeming troops nearby.

"I see it!" came the general's reply through the Titangavel. In the distance, Darius caught the flash of emerald as Maxos burst free of the front lines where skyship was coming down and raced toward it. He called out to the prince again, "Tell the men near you to get down!"

Darius bellowed over the din of the charge and ducked down low. Many of the men had already come to a stop upon seeing the crashing ship. The rest came to order on hearing his command, and dropped to their knees.

Maxos skidded to a halt right where the plummeting ship looked like it would touch down, and faced it. Darius hoped that the general knew what he was doing. If he didn't, he'd be testing the limits of the Aurora Arms' regenerative powers very soon.

Then the great wind whipped up. As Maxos lifted Watchward above his head, the gusts blew harder and harder, sending a storm of dust and grit flying where Darius and the nearby troops had hunkered down. Through the debris, he could see The Relentless' descent slowing.

A shining green light coming from Watchward drew Darius' eye to Maxos' silhouette, standing tall and resolute beneath the rocking ship. The general didn't even flinch as his tightly controlled winds bore the skyship lower and lower, setting it down gently in the cracked expanse.

The winds calmed. Through the clearing dust, Darius spied Maxos collapsed in a heap on the ground, and beyond him, the necromancer's forces receding deeper into the wastes. The prince swore, frustrated by their escape, before he rose and dashed to the general's side.

"Maxos," he called out as he dropped to his knees by the general.

Movement and a faint groan confirmed that he was alive. If Darius could come back from being pounded into the ground by a jinra, Riggs would be okay soon. It seemed like the effort of harnessing his power over storms at such a scale had exhausted him. He peered at Darius through squinted eyes. "Did I get it?"

Darius replied, relieved. "You did. Nice catch."

The general coughed a few times before nodding. "It was behind us...What hit it?"

The prince looked back to the south from where they'd come and found the answer. "Look," he said, propping Maxos up and pointing toward the horizon.

Off in the distance, a wall of glowing, misty forms stretched high into the sky and out to the east and west, gradually curving inward and sprawling on for miles with no visible end. It shined that same haunting violet color of the runes scribed upon the mummified sorcerers and emitted tormented moans that echoed across the wastes, unnerving Darius.

"What is it?" Maxos wondered.

The prince just shook his head. "Couldn't tell you," he began, "but whatever it is, it knocked The Relentless clean out of

133

the sky when it sprung up."

The Relentless. Someone needed to check on Vasna and the ship's crew to make sure they were okay. He encouraged Maxos to take his time getting up and strode toward the downed skyship.

The arcs of energy he'd seen as The Relentless had been crashing had subsided, but he still took care approaching. Parts of the ship's aft end had been sheared off, including a section of the frame encasing one of the now cracked crystal that had served as half of the vessel's propulsion. The hatch at the back of the ship had been damaged too, but the jagged gouges gave the prince a good place to grip it and tug it open with his enhanced might.

The magelamps that normally lit the inner halls of the ship were dark. Darius called out to the crew members as he entered. Weak replies echoed back from inside. He made his way toward the bridge, checking on anyone he found. Their injuries ran the spectrum from bumps and bruises to bones broken at angles that made him grimace, and he directed them toward the army's medics as he went, but didn't accompany them. He found himself mostly concerned for Vasna as he pressed on toward the upper decks.

When he finally reached the bridge, he found that the door had jammed. From behind it, he heard familiar voices.

"What was that sound?" Pierce asked sharply.

Treve's laid-back drawl reassured him. "S'the pipes, man. Take it easy. We're okay."

"But what if it's one of those skeletons *on* the pipes?"

"Then we're kinda screwed."

"You are *not* helping."

"I was kidding, man. It's the pipes. Even if it were just one of those things, Cap'n Crackshot here could turn him into spareribs. Ain't that right, Cap'n?"

Vasna spoke up. "Probably. All the same, I'd strongly prefer to not have to test your confidence."

Darius breathed a sigh of relief. They were okay. With a

strong, backhand blow, he popped it loose and sent it slamming open to find himself face-to-face with Vasna Hain, magelock pistols drawn, wide-eyed and gasping in surprise. Behind her, Pierce peeked timidly around the taller Treve.

"Stars, you scared me!" she scolded him, lowering her guns. "Do you know how close I just came to putting a couple of holes in you? I thought those horrors had boarded us!"

"Sorry, sorry." Darius resisted the urge to tell her that he doubted the attack would drop him. He found himself relieved to see that the captain hadn't suffered any major injuries. "Seems like we're safe for now, though," he added.

"For now, indeed," she countered with an exasperated sigh. "Whatever that field back there is, when it came up, it struck The Relentless hard enough to knock her out of the sky. I doubt it's any more permeable down here, which means we've got several thousand men stuck out in a lifeless wasteland with no access to a resupply."

Darius cringed. He hadn't considered the logistics until now. He didn't know how dependent Vatrisland's army was on a supply chain, but he suspected that the men carried no more than a week's rations and water with them at best. Once that was exhausted, even the most disciplined man wouldn't be able to resist fatigue for long.

They were stranded and living on borrowed time because of him. He had closed in and spooked the necromancer. He had pressed on leading the charge in spite of the Oracle's warning. He rubbed his unarmored hand over his face as the seeds of guilt took root. Some hero he was turning out to be.

Vasna looked at him again after she'd taken a moment to assess the damage on the bridge, and read his expression. "Don't get like that now. It's counterproductive," she urged him flatly.

"Yeah, thanks," the prince quipped. "I was looking for some salt to rub in this wound."

135

"Look," she shot back, giving him her full attention. "The fact of the matter is that you're stuck out here with all of these men, and as both their prince and an Aurora Knight, they're going to look to you for guidance and inspiration. If you walk out of this ship all hangdog and navel-gazing, they're going to know they can't count on you or your Knights, and then you'll really be in trouble."

"But I led the charge that got them stuck here! They probably already think I've failed them."

She crossed the space between them and leaned against a nearby railing, trying to tug her disheveled mane of hair back into place as she counseled him. "True," she conceded, "but you can't change that part. What you can still choose is whether or not you stay constructive. If you despair now, you're exactly as ruined as you think you are."

Darius didn't make eye contact. "Easy for you to say. You keep everything under control."

Vasna suddenly softened her tone. "That's not true."

When she didn't clarify, Darius looked up. Now it was the captain who refused to make eye contact. "What do you mean?" he pressed her.

She cleared her throat. "Pierce, Treve, now that the door's open, go check out the exterior damage. We need to get an idea of what repairs are going to look like."

The two crewmen nodded and made for the door, Treve offering Darius a supportive clasp on the shoulder as he passed. Once they had vacated the bridge, she closed the door behind them and looked at Darius. "Your father knows that you chose Riggs over Andler for your second."

"What?" he blurted back at her. "How?"

Vasna sighed and paced, staring at the ceiling. "I was in contact with the Oracle right before that field came up and struck The Relentless. I didn't know he was in the room with her and I brought up you and Maxos working together. I just didn't expect him to be in Aurora Tower, but there he was."

Darius clutched at his forehead in frustration. "How did he react?"

"When I said Maxos' name, your father was outraged. The Oracle looked panicked, too. That's the last thing I saw before I lost communication with them."

Darius quickly clutched the Titangavel. He had to get in touch with the tower to say his side of things. "Oracle? Oracle!" he called.

Vasna just looked down, shaking her head. "That's not going to work," she told him. "The whole reason I moved The Relentless forward was to catch up and stop you once she realized she couldn't reach you anymore." She gestured toward the magic mirror in the room. "This can't reach anyone either. We're completely cut off from home."

Darius' heart raced in his chest. His father hated the Oracle, but he wouldn't harm her, would he? Even if he thought she was advising his own son to disobey him, he'd have a rebellion in Cloudbreach on his hands if he actually hurt her somehow. The people loved the Knights. Still, he could also remember times that his father had overreacted to lesser infractions. The racing in his chest refused to calm down.

Though there was no way to be sure as to what his father would do, he had to get that barrier down. At the very least, he'd get Vatrisland's forces free and headed back to fresh supplies, but the sooner he could get the job done, the sooner he could contact the castle and take responsibility for his decision. The Oracle and the maidens shouldn't have to suffer for a choice that he owned.

"How soon do you think you can repair The Relentless in the field?" He asked Vasna.

She shook her head. "It's hard to say. Depends on how deep the fracture in the crystal is, but just based on what I can tell from here, we're at two days minimum. Mind you, that's if it's fixable and that's to get us at a speed I'd describe as 'limping.'"

Darius nodded and started swiftly striding toward the door. "I'll tell the officers and soldiers to make repairing The Relentless their top priority. Ask them for whatever you need to get the job done."

"What about you? Where are you going?" she fired back quickly.

"I'm getting Maxos and we're riding deeper into the Cryptwastes. At the very least, we need to not lose track of where that necromancer is headed. If we see an opening to take him out or we figure out how to get that barrier down too, that much the better."

"Not without me you're not."

Darius halted and faced her. The littlest twitch of annoyance gathered in his cheek, just below his eye. "I'm sure you have some extremely logical explanation as to why you're making such a crazy proposal?"

"I'm glad you asked," she fired back, not missing a beat. "There are three reasons actually. First, Pierce and Treve have the combined expertise needed to oversee every facet of this ship's maintenance, making my presence for the repairs redundant. Second, you're going into a region with an extensive and under-documented magical history, and—correct me if I'm wrong—neither you nor General Riggs, despite your incredible combined combat prowess, can tell a rune from a ward. Without support from someone with an equally extensive magical education, it's unlikely that you'll know what to do with whatever dreadful thing is hidden out there if you do find it."

Her second point got to him. All his rushing would be wasted if he came across a magical problem that couldn't be solved with a savage hammering. Still, he was curious. "And the third reason?" he reminded her with a sigh.

138

At that, Vasna whipped aside the flaps of her long coat and rested her hands on her pair of magelocks once again. "He brought down my ship," she replied. "I've decided I take that personally."

Darius snorted, offering her a half-smile. For as different as the two of them were, he kept finding himself inclined to like Vasna. She knew what she wanted, and she wasn't afraid to go after it. She spoke her mind, and cleared up misinformation quickly. The impression that he'd gotten from afar of her at the castle as a humorless genius and workaholic had been only part of the picture. Now, he was glad for an excuse to have the fiery captain beside him for the challenges ahead.

"Okay, Captain," Darius agreed. "Get yourself ready. I'll tell Maxos what's going on and we'll aim to get on our way shortly."

XXX

"Darius, this is a bad idea," Maxos said.

The prince had taken charge of three hounds whose riders had fallen in battle. He stopped tying supplies to them for a moment at Maxos' complaint. He hadn't expected the general to have any problem with Vasna coming along with them, so he hadn't bothered to tell him. Only when Maxos had asked him why he was preparing three hounds instead of two, had he explained what Vasna had said about having a magical expert with them as they went deeper into the wastes.

"Don't fight me on this, Maxos," Darius replied. "She's got a good argument. That necromancer isn't just going to have the doors thrown open for us. He's probably got all kinds of tricks and traps set up to keep us out of wherever he's hiding. She'll be able to help us get through that stuff, and she's got those two magelocks to protect herself."

"Having weapons doesn't make someone a fighter!" the

general countered. "Didn't you see how those undead thinned our numbers out here? We're down hundreds of trained soldiers after that fight. What does Captain Hain have? At best, some basic militia training from years ago, and maybe some target practice with those pistols. You'll get her killed if you take her with us, and if I understand right, she's a pretty valuable asset to your father. If you're looking to piss him off, you've found a nice shortcut."

It was a little too late to avoid doing that, Darius thought to himself. He sighed. "So what do you suggest?"

"We've got to go at this more carefully," Maxos advised him. "If we take the remaining men forward and engage on favorable terrain, they can keep the necromancer's forces occupied while I scout things out. I'm as fast as lightning, Darius. Literally. If you and the troops keep his forces off of me, I can assess whatever place they've fallen back to. Then, we withdraw to a safe distance and look at the new information."

The prince shook his head. "That's going to be too time consuming. This guy drew us back, trapped us here, and then ran away. He wants our forces this close for something, and every second we wait, he's getting closer to pulling whatever it is he wants to do. If we go back and forth like you want to, we blow a lot of time that we can't guarantee we have."

"That's conjecture!" the general shot back, nearly cutting Darius off. "Listen to yourself. Something? Whatever? Might? You're making this call based on guesses. We need real, solid information. We can't just assault his lair with all of these men and hope they come out okay."

"Well," Darius admitted to Maxos, "at least that's one thing we agree on."

The general cocked his head to one side. Then he widened his eyes. "You can't possibly be suggesting that just the three of us go in."

Darius shrugged, cinching a pack more tightly to one of the

hounds. "The high general agreed with you. He said he'd rather face court martial for defying the prince than go along with my plan. I get it, though. I got Vatrisland's men into this situation. I got them trapped out here on limited supplies at the mercy of a madman. I won't ask anything more of them until I can redeem myself. We'll go, just the three of us, and we'll stay light and fast. Might not involve as much facing things head-on as I'd like, but it doesn't risk any more soldiers' lives."

Maxos looked down, shaking his head. "This too reckless. You're acting crazy."

"We're stronger than you think, Maxos. We can do this," Darius insisted.

"You're ignoring the size of that army," the general argued. "This is unprecedented necromantic power at work and you just want to hit-and-run with two Knights and a hobbyist gunslinger? It's suicide!"

Darius ignored him. He'd already failed the men who'd been withered or gutted by the undead army. Now he fixed his mind on the needs of the ones he could still help. Without supplies coming in, the men who remained would find themselves rationing their water over the next few days to hold out as long as they could. If the Aurora Arms were as powerful as everyone believed they were, he and Maxos would be able to stop the necromancer. After seeing the general draw on Watchward's power to save The Relentless, he knew that he could push the Titangavel's powers further too. He just had to try harder.

"Am I interrupting something?" Vasna asked, arriving with a small satchel of personal supplies.

Maxos frowned at her. "This is hardly sensible, Captain. You never struck me as being this imprudent."

"General," Vasna replied confidently, "I take full responsibility for my own well-being in this endeavor. If there's one thing you can depend on, I will never ask either of you to coddle me. But make no mistake. You do need my expertise to face what's ahead. You two do what you do best, and I'll do the same."

The general shook his head in disbelief as Darius and Vasna mounted up on their hounds. Darius looked down from his dog at Maxos and offered, "If you don't want to come, I'll understand."

Maxos shook his head. "Offering a man a choice to act against every fiber of his being isn't really offering him a choice at all," he answered as he mounted the third hound. "You know full well that I'll do my duty as a Knight."

Darius nodded. A part of him wanted to keep trying to justify his decision to his companion, but he knew it would be a waste of breath. He'd prove himself to Maxos by bringing in results. As they rode off to the north in pursuit of the undead horde, he tried to comfort himself with the thought that all leaders made calls that their subordinates questioned from time to time. He couldn't possibly please everyone all of the time.

He took a look back at the soldiers setting up camp and hunkering down as he and his allies turned to ride into the wastes. Among them stood General Andler, who happened to lock eyes with him. The General looked profoundly defeated, shoulders slumped and expression sagging. Darius hadn't pegged him to be the despairing type when the going got rough. What had gotten to the hardened officer?

He turned his eyes to the trail ahead for only a moment before he knew. He'd looked like he'd been preparing three dogs for two Knights. When Vasna had mounted up alongside them, Andler's highest hope had been dashed. That had to be it.

The prince looked back one more time, but the general had vanished among the soldiers.

142

13

Any effort Ria made to encourage her maidens couldn't seem to overcome the somber air that cloaked Aurora Tower the day after they lost contact with the Knights. On top of having no way to get in touch with Darius and the others out in the Cryptwastes, King Magnus' last menacing words before he had left the tower still hung over all of them. Though she knew he couldn't act against her openly, Ria knew she hadn't had the last of her trouble with him.

With the mood of the other women beginning to dampen her own spirits, the Oracle removed herself from the tower and walked the gardens surrounding the castle clutching a rough blanket and a small satchel of books and notes that her maidens had set aside for her. Here she could recompose herself in private. She had to appear strong in front of them.

The garden's carefully trimmed hedges and barely budding spring flowers spread out before her. Nobles in pairs and trios walked the broad, open spaces that acted as hubs, branching to quiet, secluded nooks that offered a more intimate space. Upon finding a quiet spot to herself, she spread her blanket beneath an old pine tree and settled in comfortably. She allowed herself only a few moments to quietly enjoy the sunshine and fresh air before she undid the latch on her satchel and spread her maidens' research out before her.

They had narrowed their search to some promising leads based on the descriptions Darius and Maxos had sent back from the field. According to their notes, the distinctive cobra motif jewelry that the Knights had seen on members of the undead army had grown popular in the last few decades prior to the Blightfire. The style had started among the royalty and well-to-dos as a symbol of fervent patriotism, and had gradually spread down to the common people.

The notes on jewelry directed Ria to reference an account of a traveler who had traveled through Anceda Pryta less than a year prior to the Blightfire. She smiled when she pulled out the referenced work and noticed whose writings she'd be studying next.

"Min's Ramble" was a collection of personal diaries written by Aurora Knight Min Leffant. Min's insatiable curiosity led her to strike out on her own with Feygrip at her side, much to the irritation of her Knight-Captain. History, however, validated Min's wanderlust. The detailed accounts of her journeys had helped three generations of Knights avert terrible crises.

Was Min's legacy about to strike for a fourth time? Ria paged eagerly to the bookmarked entry and began to read.

I'm glad that I decided to disguise myself as an Itradi scholar with Feygrip before I entered Anceda Pryta. Looks like the Empire's open hostility toward Vatrisland has transferred to the Aurora Knights by association. The commoners I've spoken to are firmly convinced that it's only a matter of time before we reveal that our true loyalties lie with their neighbor, and not with the good of the world.

I'll readily admit that having the Aurora Arms housed in Vatrisland has inspired the people there, but we have no bias favoring Vatrisland. I just wish I had some kind of proof I could show these scared people.

Unfortunately, the nobility here aren't helping the situation. Official addresses refer to us as a special wing of

Vatrisland's military, and warn that no one can truly rest easy until their own defenders can match the Knights' powers. It's whipped these people into a hard working frenzy to outpace Vatrisland's recent developments, and it's made them paranoid.

Take these "marks of loyalty" that they're all wearing, for example. They're pendants shaped like the head of a cobra. I was reminded as soon as I entered the city that I wasn't wearing one. I promised that I'd get one as soon as I had a moment to spare, but got distracted by other things. Soon, I noticed a steadily growing crowd of uniquely uniformed guards hovering near me no matter which part of town I visited. They continued to follow me around until I got and wore a pendant of my own.

The commoners relaxed around me a bit more after that. I asked them about this special guard squadron. They are the Orben'rata; guards who investigate suspected disloyalty to the Itradi Emperor in the capital.

Needless to say, it's all pretty troubling. I'll be contacting Aurora Tower this evening with my observations. Maybe the shrine maidens will be able to cross-reference this with another incident.

Ria read over the passage again. Manipulated commoners, cult-like behavior, loyalty police. But there was something else off about the entry that she couldn't seem to put her finger on during her initial reading.

Orben'rata.

The word didn't sound Itradi to her, and Min hadn't provided a translation. She'd been in the field, so she wouldn't have had access to study aids to help her. Ria, however, was better equipped. She spent the next several minutes breaking the name down into root words with her resources.

A dead end. The word had no meaning. To the Itradi, it would have sounded like nothing more than a random collection of syllables.

Min had no doubt run the word by her shrine maidens when she'd reported in, but later entries in the Knight's journal didn't indicate that she'd ever gotten a translation. Ria could only assume that the shrine didn't have an answer.

Or hadn't had an answer at the time.

"Dawntongue," Ria murmured. It was an obscure language that had only been discovered within the last hundred years. Scholars had made contact with small pockets of jungle-dwelling tribesmen living near the equator, and had deciphered their language after Min's time.

Realizing she'd need to head back to the tower for more resources, Ria set her current books aside and sighed. She just had to be patient. Whatever empowered their foe out in the Cryptwastes could be extremely obscure, but Aurora Tower had accumulated incredible amounts of lore over the centuries. Between her own resources, and those in the castle's library, surely she and her maidens could find a way to support the Knights.

"There you are!"

Ria jerked her head up, startled to see her aide hustling over from the garden's central path. "Goodness, Charise. I didn't hear you come up."

"Sorry, Miss Ria," the girl explained. "I've just been looking all over for you."

Ria touched her hand to her chest, trying to still her racing heart. Her arguments with Magnus had set her more on edge than she thought. On top of that, now she looked shaken in front of one of her maidens. It was hardly leader-like. She took a deep breath, regaining her composure. "What brings you out here? You're the first maiden I've seen outside of the tower all day."

"Something happened, so I came to look for you," Charise went on quietly. "Good thing the maidens at the tower's doors saw you head off this way. I'd never have thought to look for you here."

Now Ria noticed the girl's expression clouded with worry. Mentally, she scolded herself for hiding away so selfishly when she was needed. "Come, sit. Tell me what's going on," she said, gathering and stacking her books neatly before giving the girl her full attention.

Charise seated herself. She glanced around the garden at nobles in the distance for a moment, then began to speak quietly. "We won't be getting the offering from the other shrines this month. I managed to listen in on King Magnus speaking with some of the other nobles. He's detained the pilgrims and the shipment that they were escorting. They're accused of conspiracy to undermine the crown."

"Impossible," Ria insisted. "What reason would our volunteers have to try to hurt Vatrisland?"

The girl looked down as she continued. "That's just it," she said. "They didn't even do anything. He had his guards plant false evidence at a checkpoint when the pilgrims entered the city."

Ria scowled. This stung more than Magnus going after her directly. She had the guts and the status to push back against him. The Knights' pilgrims didn't have the same advantages.

The young maiden shook her head, continuing to look down. "King Magnus is holding them to hurt us. This is just the beginning, Miss Ria. He bragged to the other men that he would see you and the Aurora Knights ruined. That as you had turned his son against him, he would turn the world against you."

"Mm. And I don't suppose he's interested in hearing that I've done nothing of the sort," Ria mused. Darius really had freely chosen Riggs for his second, even after Magnus had bribed him, but how could she convince the king of the truth? She didn't imagine he'd be very receptive to an audience with her now.

So this was it then. Not only did she have a danger in the Cryptwastes to contend with, but she could no longer hope to just tolerate Magnus or find compromise with him. She struggled to decide which problem she should tackle first. The pilgrims he'd imprisoned to spite her most deserved her efforts, but with Aurora Tower's offerings cut off, the needs of her maidens would have to be addressed as well. Though they'd endure using portions of their own stipends for food, she'd have to ration the Tower's resources without a collection.

Charise broke through the silence. "It's bad, isn't it? It's really bad."

"Well, yes," Ria admitted, pausing before she added, "but we wouldn't even have the luxury of worry had you not taken on this task. How did you get close enough to hear all of this?"

Charise flushed suddenly at her question. "Well, I mean, I have to get creative right? These are big, important things that I'm trying to hear, a-and the castle isn't as friendly to us as it used to be."

Ria arched an eyebrow. "After a start like that, you can't just not tell me. Come on now, out with it."

She bobbled her head around a bit as she seemed to search for the right words. "Let's just say, I think the assistant librarian might like me."

The Oracle raised her brow higher. "Who are you and what have you done with my Charise?" she quipped. They both laughed, but she added more seriously, "Are you still being careful, though? You're doing a great service for the Knights, and I know that I can't hope for your efforts to be without risk, but there's a fine line between bravery and foolishness."

Charise nodded. "I'm being careful," she assured Ria. "I mean, he keeps walking past my table and seeing if I need anything. It's weird. Flattering too, I guess, but I keep reminding myself that I'm there for a purpose. And all we've really done is make small talk anyway. Then yesterday he just decided on his own to tell the guards that I wasn't around when I was studying in a back room, so I always make sure to smile and say hello to him

148

whenever he passes now."

The girl had turned out to be so cunning. Maybe it really was, like the old saying went, always the quiet ones. This little seed of boldness had been within her, waiting to bloom. Who knew what other buried talents the girl might reveal in time?

Perhaps she could even be the next Oracle of the Arms.

But Ria didn't need to commit to that just yet.

"Well, do remember your vows," she reminded her pupil. "And be aware of your heart. You may feel like you have your emotions under control about this librarian for now, but these things can change in the blink of an eye if you are not careful. When I was your age, I saw many a senior maiden lose her position before she intended to leave it."

Charise gave a tight-lipped smirk. "I'm not sure I can promise you I'll be careful enough times that you'll believe me, Miss Ria."

"Well, honestly, probably not," Ria confessed. "I'll try with all I have to trust you, though."

"Don't try, okay? Succeed," the girl mimicked her mentor playfully.

The Oracle raised her hands in surrender. "Okay, okay. That one was fair, I suppose," she conceded with a smile. She'd expected to lift her spirits by hiding away from everything for a while. How wrong she'd been. "Come. Let's get back to the tower and start looking into ways to get those pilgrims of ours out of the dungeons. I think I've found what I came out here for."

14

The prince and his companions rode on for two days. He'd hoped that they would catch up to the force sooner, but as the first night began to fall, none of them could even see their foes on the horizon. Vasna was quick to remind him that though they needed to stop for sleep, the undead were tireless, and likely made much better time than they did. Luckily, the broad trail that their enemy had left behind proved easy for Maxos to track. Whether the trail was too large and too difficult to mask, or the necromancer just didn't care if he was being followed, none of them knew. All the same, Darius felt grateful to have a clear direction through the miles of flats and ruins.

After their second night of travel, the group noticed that the remains of buildings and roads that they passed were in better condition the further they went. Before long, a huge, cream-white ziggurat on the horizon confirmed what Darius had begun to suspect. Their trail would come to an end in Anceda Pryta, the former capital of the Itradi Empire.

The dogs loped onward, loyally obeying their riders' commands, but Darius could tell that the Cryptwastes were taxing the beasts. Fine dust coated them all the way up their legs to their bellies, and he'd felt his own mount stepping more gingerly all morning. As they passed through a crumbling gateway into the city, he began to look out for a safe place to hitch them up far from wandering undead.

"I don't like this," Maxos murmured. "We've come a long

way without running into any undead. We should have seen something by now."

As the group pressed their mounts to crest the next hilltop, the scene that extended out before them justified Maxos' anxiety. The three quickly tugged their mounts to a stop in the middle of the road, backed them up, and urged them to lay down just out of sight. Then they crawled up to the top of the hill better examine the situation.

In the shadow of the royal ziggurat, milling around among the larger, stonework buildings that had once been part of a bustling city center, shambled thousands upon thousands of undead. The horde that had battled Vatrisland's army had been intimidating enough, but here, at least five times as many skeletal and mummified forms roamed about like bees in a hive, each seeming oblivious of the others as he wandered.

"Stars," Darius murmured. "There's probably as many here as there are men in Vatrisland's whole army."

Maxos grunted in agreement. "And where there are that many undead, that necromancer can't be far away. It's gonna be really rough getting past them all."

"Maybe not," Vasna whispered. "Look at them all. There's no order to their movements. Nobody's actively commanding them. All they'll have to work with are their dulled instincts. They won't be able to work as a group like they did when we fought them before."

Darius looked the mass of bodies over again. Sure enough, they seemed to be bumping into one another and tottering about aimlessly. He was relieved that Vasna had come along. He'd never have known to look for that tell. "That's something in our favor at least. Let's get the dogs hitched up somewhere so we can start looking for a way in."

The three crawled back from the hill and stood once they were sure that they couldn't be seen from below. A search of the

151

nearby buildings revealed one structure in which part of the first floor had collapsed into the basement. The double-wide doorway into it offered enough room for the hounds to enter. With some coaxing, Darius and Maxos managed to convince all three dogs to creep down a slanted portion of the collapsed floor into the lower level.

The riders each took several minutes to feed and water their mounts. While they all agreed that they weren't particularly excited to be hiding the hounds in a dilapidated building, they couldn't risk leaving them somewhere outside where the undead might easily find them.

With that point of logistics behind them, the three took to circling the ziggurat at a distance in search of the safest approach. Unfortunately, the crowd was about equally deep on all sides.

As they made their way through another alleyway toward the next broad avenue, Maxos came to a stop at the front of the group and peeked around, scanning down the road. After a moment, he turned back and addressed his companions. "I think I just spotted our best route. Take a look."

Darius moved up beside the general and looked ahead with him. Maxos continued, pointing into the distance as he explained, "See that aqueduct there? It goes right into the side of the ziggurat there, but follow it out a ways."

Darius followed the long trough of stone out from the structure with his eyes. It ended suddenly a few hundred feet away where a portion had collapsed, and that point was far from the mass of undead at the city's center. "I gotcha. So we get up on there and stay low on our way in. None of the guys down below get alerted. Good eye."

The three moved in via the alleyways, getting as close as they could to their destination while staying inconspicuous. Once they were under the far edge of the aqueduct, Vasna threw her arms over Darius' shoulders. "Up we go then," she said flatly.

Darius cleared his throat as she climbed onto his back. In spite of the need for haste, he couldn't help but enjoy the moment. He'd admired her from afar as he'd checked in on the construction of The Relentless before. That had been back when he'd had a simpler idea of who she was.

Now, as she pressed herself against him, he found himself hurriedly reclassifying her in his head.

After a moment, she seemed satisfied that her grip on him was secure and stopped wriggling. Darius cleared his throat and focused. "Okay, hold tight," he urged her. "Are we all clear, Maxos?"

The general peeked around the corners one last time and gave a thumbs-up. The two Knights launched into the air toward the aqueduct's ledge with Vasna in tow. Darius had instinctively compensated well for the different load on his muscles, and the group sailed quietly up into the trough, save for the soft crunch of dirt and pebbles on their landing.

Vasna slid off of Darius' back once they touched down and all three crouched low. "How'd we do?" she asked.

Maxos peeked over the side down toward the horde. "I think we're good. They aren't acting any differently. Let's stay low and get moving."

Each of them stayed crouched and stepped lightly as they padded their way along the dry trough. Before long, they were traveling over the heads of the undead, and they slowed themselves. No sense in risking any noises caused by moving quickly. Though none of them dared to look down, the unnerving din of clattering bones as skeletons shuffled and collided was all that Darius needed to hear to understand their position.

"We're almost there," he whispered, looking ahead to where the aqueduct ended into the ziggurat. A series of metal bars blocked the passage ahead, but he had no doubt that he could make short work of them with his enhanced strength or the Titangavel.

But what was that faint light beyond the bars, growing brighter?

"Look out!" Darius shouted, forgetting their cautious silence as he dove flat to the ground only a moment before a cluster of wispy, violet forms rushed over his head, crying tormented moans as they passed.

He rolled over onto his back and checked behind him. Maxos and Vasna had dropped to their bellies. They seemed to be okay, so he turned his eyes to the sky to spot the phantasmal forms arcing around and coming back toward them. He swore, rolled to his feet, and pulled the Titangavel free from the straps lashing it to his back. His allies stayed prone, drawing their weapons.

The fastest wailing form crossed into Darius' reach and he let loose with a mighty swing. Though the creature seemed misty and insubstantial, the Titangavel still connected with it, offering the kind of resistance Darius imagined he might get had he swung through jam as the spirit burst and dissipated.

Two more forms closed in, but now Maxos and Vasna had both managed to sit up and find their aim. Each fired, Maxos with his crackling arrows of lightning and Vasna with white magical shots from her magelocks. The phantoms tried to dodge and weave, but the shots struck true, riddling and ruining their targets.

With his focus no longer fixed on the spirits, Darius' mind suddenly registered chaotic sounds coming from below. He dared to peek over the edge to see the horde of undead, now frenzied and rampaging. They clawed at the pillars holding up the aqueduct, climbing on top of one another three and four high to reach the sounds of life above them. Further away, a mummified warbeast reared back and charged in their direction too.

"Move!" the prince shouted. Maxos bolted past him. Vasna threw her arms around Darius' shoulders again and he broke into a run too. They weren't far from that barred passage, but any distance would be too far until the horde lost their trail.

An explosive impact rocked the trough sharply to one side beneath Darius' feet, tossing him off balance. The shift threw him to the ground and Vasna's hands slipped free as the structure dipped downward sharply and shook with a deafening crash. He caught a rough, broken edge in the stonework to keep from sliding down and rolled to his back to see what had happened. A huge chunk of the aqueduct had split away and fallen. The warbeast bucked and struggled beside where a supporting pillar had been, spilling rubble from side-to-side. The now cocked section of the ancient structure sloped directly into the horde. Though many of the undead were crushed beneath the falling debris, plenty more surged into the chaos.

"Vasna!" Darius shouted. He'd lost track of her, and the cloud rising from the collapsed section obscured his vision.

"Darius!" Her call came from below along with the crack-fire of her pistols. Squinting, he could see her black coat flapping back and forth wildly through the dust. Instantly, he released his grip and slid toward her, using his momentum to kick up onto his feet and into a breakneck downhill sprint. A barrage of Maxos' now-familiar lightning arrows ripped past him as he ran, clearing the front most line of enemies.

The prince roared as he leapt into the fray, lashing out with wild swings of the Titangavel. Showers of bony shards scattered into the sky with each blow. The quick mummified sorcerers lurched toward him too, but seeing Vasna in peril had focused him. He precisely compensated for each weave and sway. For all that the undead tried, they might just as well have faced a wall of solid steel. None made it any closer than his furthest reach with the Titangavel.

"Go! I've got them!" Darius commanded Vasna. Behind him, he could hear her coughing and scrambling her way up the slope. He didn't dare take his eyes off of the approaching horrors. Every instinct he had translated instantly into action as he crushed more of them from every angle.

"Give me your hand!" Maxos shouted from behind him. He was too far away to be talking to Darius. He'd likely come to aid Vasna. That was one problem solved, but the other remained. For every foe he downed another took its place. He needed to cut off their path to his party, or at least buy time to get everyone into the ziggurat and beyond pursuit.

At that moment, as if in response to his desire to save and protect his friends, an otherworldly calm fell over Darius. Incredible might surged up his arms and throughout his every muscle from the Titangavel, and his actions were no longer his own. He watched his arms raise the Titangavel high above his head and slam it down on the ground in front of him.

A wake of absolute destruction ripped forth from the point of impact. Though the ground beneath his feet remained still and unaffected, the earth in front of Darius churned like water for a hundred yards out in a perfect half-circle from where he stood. Building after building crashed in on itself as though it were made of toy blocks. The roads ripped from the ground in chunks that turned end-over-end like autumn leaves caught in the wind, crashing down on the hundreds of undead unlucky enough to be in the blast radius. Just outside of that precisely shaped zone of unnatural disaster, the ziggurat and closest section of aqueduct on which his friends stood remained completely unharmed.

A great cloud of dust rose from the wrecked cityscape. Before it obscured his vision, Darius spotted the remaining undead in the distance, struggling fruitlessly against the maze of debris he'd left.

Then the cloud covered him.

XXX

Muffled voices droned over and over, penetrating the heavy

fog of unconsciousness that wrapped around Darius. Slowly, they became clearer and clearer, and harsh sunlight glowed through his eyelids, forcing a squint of protest. His heartbeat drummed loudly in his head and every muscle in his arms protested as he brought his hands up to clutch his temples. Though every part of him ached, consciousness seemed less an enemy as the moments passed, and soon he was able to open his eyes.

Maxos' voice was the first to come in clearly. "Hey, he's back with us."

"Darius, you did it," came Vasna's next.

The relieved smiles of his allies drifted into focus, as did his surroundings. The three of them were tucked tightly into the same barred passageway he'd seen earlier at the end of the aqueduct.

"I did it?" Darius groaned, blinking and squinting. The throbbing in his head was beginning to fade.

Vasna nodded. "I've never seen anything like it. Look." She helped tilt him so he could see the city below out of the passage.

He surveyed the aftermath of his battle. From their vantage point partway up the ziggurat, the sight was even more astounding than what he'd taken in from the ground. A whole city block had collapsed into tunnels below the street. At the furthest edges of the devastation, a few figures from the horde had made it ten or twenty yards in, but they kept having to stop to search for paths around the gaping pits and heaps of rubble he'd left behind. He took comfort that they didn't seem to be particularly deep thinkers. It would take them quite a while to get anywhere near him and his friends, but he wouldn't spare them any of that time.

"Let's keep moving," Darius grunted, pushing himself to his feet. He only stayed upright for a moment before dizziness dropped him back to his knees.

"Easy, Darius," Maxos warned him. "It took me several

minutes after I gave it my all too. Just breathe for a bit. You gave them plenty of trouble to sort out down there."

The prince resisted the urge to protest further and let the power of the Titangavel continue its work refreshing him. In the quiet, he thought back on the moments that had led up to him unleashing that earthquake. He faced Maxos and asked, "When you made that twister that caught The Relentless, did you feel like you...." He trailed off briefly, searching for the right words. "...Weren't yourself when you did it?"

Maxos watched the creatures working their way through the wreckage below as he replied. "I did. I honestly didn't know how I would stop the ship when I dashed out there, but as soon as I was in the right spot, something just took over. It was like I just knew what to do."

Darius looked down at the Titangavel resting at his side. No one had ever mentioned such a thing in any of the legends he'd read. Was it some secret knowledge that the Knights had carefully guarded, or was this the first time such a thing had happened? The more he thought over the moment, reliving that other will tugging on his limbs, the more it unnerved him. He gripped the Titangavel and called out to the Oracle to ask her about it.

That was right. They were separated from her. There would be no asking for encouragement, let alone information, from anyone. He'd feared that her constant presence would hamper his ability to lead and make his own judgments before. Now, as he and his friends prepared to descend into the ziggurat, he wished for a moment that he had someone to whom he could defer.

Stars. He'd even settle for his father now.

He would ask the Oracle about the strange sensation once he returned to Cloudbreach. People were counting on him right now. Getting any further lost in thought about it would have to wait.

Another minute passed, and the prince felt steady enough to

stand under his own power. "Okay, let's figure out what's hiding in here," he said. He slipped his hands between the vertical bars that blocked their path and wrenched them outward, bending them to create an entrance. The three slipped through the opening and into the halls of the royal ziggurat.

15

"Stars, Charise, did you sleep at all?"

Ria stepped into the top chamber of Aurora Tower to find Charise hunched in the exact seat where she'd left her the night before.

The girl looked up from the scattered books and documents on Vatrisland's legal code, squinting. "Oh, good morning Miss Ria," she said slowly before cocking her head to glance out a nearby window. "Wow. No, I guess I didn't."

The Oracle furrowed her brow in worried sympathy. The two of them had been refused visitation with the pilgrims King Magnus had imprisoned, and so had searched late into the night for some way to have them released. Ria had succumbed to the need for sleep sometime after midnight and dismissed herself. Charise had told her that she would clean up their study space and get some rest too, but apparently the girl's youthful vigor had carried her through the night.

"Can you even see straight anymore?" Ria asked, walking over to the table and seating herself. "Understanding the nuances of legal code is hard enough for the uninitiated on a full night of sleep. You won't be much help to those pilgrims if you can't understand what you're reading."

Charise sighed in frustration. "The sad thing is, Miss Ria, I do understand it. At least enough to know we don't have any recourse. Normally it would be on the accusers to prove the pilgrims' guilt, but it's different with the King. He's not held to the same rules."

"And even if he were, all we have is what you overheard in the castle," Ria murmured.

The two of them sat in silence for the moment. Even with the bits of intelligence Charise could gather by snooping around the castle, at the end of the day, they were still fighting against a man with an entire nation of resources at his command. Ria scowled. "What about that odd word that I gave you yesterday? Did it make any sense in Dawntongue?"

The girl nodded grimly as she pawed through her books and notes for a moment. Eventually, she fished out a sheet covered in her handwriting. "Orben'rata does have a meaning in Dawntongue: 'Ruiner's Servants.'"

"Ruiner's servants?" Ria echoed. She stared off into the distance as the first frighteningly likely possible meaning came to mind. "The Harbinger of Ruin," she murmured.

If she was right, she would be remembered as fully justified in calling together a team of Aurora Knights, but that was little comfort. The Harbingers were great beasts of terrible power, locked away in another reality ages ago according to various oral histories. If one had returned to their world, even a full team of Knights would be hard pressed to seal it away again, much less kill it.

Charise hesitated before nodding. "It does seem the most likely when you put it together."

"And if that's the case," Ria went on, "either the Orben'rata were the Harbinger's thralls, or they were commanded by someone else who was. Maybe even the Itradi Emperor himself."

"And that would explain the things you mentioned from Min's account," Charise added, wide-eyed. "The paranoia, the sudden advancements in their magecraft. They were dealing for power with a force they didn't understand."

"Perhaps even the Blightfire, hm? The power of a

Harbinger gone horribly out of control? It would fit with the magnitude of the disaster." It was only theory, of course, but Ria shook her head, dismayed at how much sense it all made.

Faint music in the distance interrupted her thoughts. Ria listened for a moment, trying to hear it more clearly.

"Trumpets," Charise observed. "Coming from the castle."

"Somebody's making an announcement," Ria said with a nod. "Come. Let's see what this is about."

XXX

The two women exited Aurora Tower to find the approach to the castle teeming with soldiers as townsfolk began to pour through the outer gates. A substantial military presence for an announcement wasn't entirely unusual. Soldiers always helped control crowds at these sorts of events, and made sure that no curious citizens or ambitious thieves tried to sneak into the castle using the audience as a distraction. The events of the past several days, though, had prepared Ria to expect the worst, and she didn't dare cast aside the unease that fell over her as she watched the people gather.

Before long, the better part of the courtyard was packed shoulder-to-shoulder with people from every walk of life. Attendance for these kinds of announcements wasn't mandatory. After all, not every man could set down his job in the middle of the morning and run off to the castle. There were always enough curious citizens, however, to ensure that the king's message would be heard and spread throughout the city.

King Magnus took position on the castle balcony to the wild cheers of his subjects. Ria bit her lip and remained silent. They didn't know how he really was, but how could they? All they ever got to see was his public persona, and Magnus manipulated their military pride well. Clad in his shining ceremonial armor, he looked as much warrior as king.

"Fellow noblemen, revered soldiers, and citizens of Cloudbreach," he began, "I come before you today to prepare you for a time of change. What I am about to say may fill you with concern, but I bring you this news myself, that I might ease your fears and have your understanding.

"Yesterday, we took into custody a group of spies discovered to be posing as pilgrims escorting offerings to Aurora Tower. Our able soldiers discovered their ruse and isolated them before they could enact any of their nefarious plans to undermine our great kingdom!"

The crowd erupted into a cheer of approval. Charise paled. "Lies! He's lying," she hissed quietly to Ria. The Oracle looked around at the crowd nervously. If anyone had heard the girl over the roar of approval, they weren't acting on it.

"However," King Magnus went on, "in the course of interrogating these knaves, we were able to discover that they planned to deliver a message to a co-conspirator already hidden among us.

"A spy already stationed right there," he roared, pointing across the courtyard, "in our beloved Aurora Tower!"

Concerned chatter crisscrossed the crowd.

"When our interrogators extracted this information from the prisoners, they immediately set to task on discovering the identity of this traitor in our midst, but unfortunately, our captives managed to end their lives like the cowards they were before the truth could be revealed."

Ria and Charise looked at one another, each matching the other's look of disbelief. "He killed them," the girl mouthed at her mentor. The Oracle nodded subtly in response. Fiery anger seeped in to replace the chill of fear in her core, and she balled her hands into fists to contain it.

"Now I know that all of you, as I do, take great pride in our

163

great capital being home to Aurora Tower and the Arms housed within. Though the Aurora Knights are not governed by Vatrisland, we have been close allies these past thousand years, and that is due, in no small part, to our capacity to compromise, and to respect one another's privacy. But this situation demands that I make Vatrisland's safety my highest priority.

"Therefore, starting tomorrow, until we successfully root out this conspirator who threatens everything we hold dear, Vatrisland's soldiers will occupy Aurora Tower alongside its residents."

Magnus' words hammered down on Ria like boulders in a landslide. He couldn't do it. At least he couldn't do it for long. The explanation he'd given had likely struck enough fear into his own people to placate them, but Vatrisland's neighbors would surely condemn it. Did he just think that there was nothing that they could do to stop him? Or did he hope to accomplish something before the other rulers had time to collaborate on some formal, concrete opposition?

The king continued, "Only by thoroughly investigating Aurora Tower can we close the net on a cowardly foe who subverts its independent status to hide from justice. Soon, fellow Vatrislanders, we will drive out the conspirators that threaten us, and ensure the security of our interests."

"Miss Ria." Charise shook her arm. "I think we'd better go."

The Oracle looked around at her aide's prompting. Though much of the audience had applauded and cheered at King Magnus' declaration, those nearby had begun to turn their attention to her. She didn't see any malice or threat in their expressions, but they looked to be reading her; gauging her reaction to the announcement.

"Indeed," she agreed quietly. Shoulder-to-shoulder within a crowd composed of the king's most loyal followers was no place

164

to take an official position on his announcement.

16

By entering the royal ziggurat the way that they had, Darius, Maxos, and Vasna had bypassed the upper levels. Together they crept through the complex infrastructure that had once made this the most sophisticated building in the city, guided through the darkness by the softly glowing Aurora Arms. The path of the aqueduct had split into smaller troughs that spread throughout the interior once they had gotten well inside, and now they searched the meandering, filthy halls for a hint as to what the right direction might be.

The search eventually brought them to a pair of staircases. Vasna was the first to offer insight. "Well, down then obviously?" she asked, breathing heavily as she descended.

Darius didn't follow. "Obviously?" he asked, genuinely curious. "Why not up?"

"Think about how high on the structure we were when we entered. If he were above, we'd have come across defenses of some kind by now, unless he's only using a tiny part of the building," Vasna explained. "Below us, on the other hand, there's a whole lot of ziggurat left to explore."

Darius glanced at Maxos, who looked unsurprised. The prince nodded and suppressed a wince as they moved on down the staircase. For all of the effort he put forth to be a leader, he struggled with these finer points of strategy and intelligence. Maybe this was just another one of those things that the Oracle had anticipated when she'd encouraged him to recruit help quickly.

Vasna had actually been quite helpful so far. He'd expected Maxos to hold his own as a general bearing one of the Aurora Arms, but Vasna, even without those blessings, had been quick on her feet and quicker still on the draw when she'd needed to fight.

He took a few longer strides to get up alongside her. "Hey," he began quietly, "you're really showing Maxos, huh?"

"Oh?" She seemed distracted as she answered. "How do you mean?"

"Just the way that he was dead set against you coming. How he was worried that you'd get into trouble. You've been a good fighter, though. You're a real crack shot with those magelock things."

"Don't be silly, Darius," she said with a nervous laugh. "I'm not here to show anyone up. I'm just glad that I can help the Knights."

Darius furrowed his brow. This humility was out of character for the normally more fiery Vasna. She wasn't making eye contact with him either, instead favoring a gaze straight ahead. In the dim light, he could see beads of sweat gathered on her forehead near her temple.

"You seem nervous. Something wrong?" he pressed bluntly.

"What? No, nothing's wrong."

"You can tell me. What is it? Darkness? Spiders? Tight spaces?"

"Darius, there is nothing wrong," she snapped, facing him. "I'm just a little winded. That's all."

"Okay, I'll let it go," he surrendered. Something was putting her off, though. She definitely was afraid. With each day she spent outside of her tightly controlled workshop back at Cloudbreach, she seemed a little more human.

"This looks promising," Maxos chimed in. He'd slipped ahead while they'd been talking, and now stood in a doorway just ahead of them.

The three gathered at the threshold and the Knights held their weapons aloft, extending the light out further. They had entered a vast room filled with tables, tools, and half constructed magecraft apparatuses. It looked like some kind of workshop with enough space to employ hundreds of craftsmen at once.

Vasna strode over to a table, tugging Darius along to have light with her. She looked wide-eyed at the tools and gadgets spread out before her, picking them up one after another and brushing the dust off of them to examine details. Maxos peered into the dark corners of the chamber with Watchward at the ready as he followed close behind them.

"What is this stuff?" Darius asked Vasna.

"It looks Itradi, but that's impossible," she replied, still staring at the objects.

Darius urged her to continue. "What do you mean?"

She plucked one of the tools from the table and held it up for Darius to see. While he had to admit that he wasn't particularly familiar with the tools of the magecraft trade, there certainly didn't seem to be anything special about the dusty cylinder rod with a small crystal mounted upon it.

"This," she explained, "is a harmonizer. It's a magecraft tool that helps craftsmen align multiple crystals to work together. If you use it correctly, you can link crystals to get a multiplicative power output instead of an additive one. We use something like this in my workshop today."

"So what's so surprising about finding one here?" Darius asked.

Vasna rubbed her chin thoughtfully with her free hand as she went on. "We didn't come up with these in Vatrisland until about two hundred years ago. That's about four hundred years after the Itradi Empire fell, which means one of two things as far as I can guess. Either people were still working here long after the

168

Blightfire leveled the empire, or the Itradi somehow got far ahead of their time in magecraft before they died."

"What about the necromancer?" Maxos asked, "Couldn't he have just brought this stuff out here?"

Vasna shook her head, tracing a finger over some odd, acute angles near the tool's head. "It wouldn't explain why the tool has these Itradi decorative flourishes, see? This has similar styling to the stonework on some of the later buildings outside. Furthermore, there would be no point in using something this ancient today when more modern alternatives exist. This was ahead of its time, sure, but it's nothing compared to the ones we use now."

"Okay, I'm sure this is all very exciting for the history books, but can we do something practical with it?" Darius piped back in. "Because if not, we should get moving."

"It is practical, Darius," Vasna insisted sharply, turning her harsh glare on him. "We've never discovered the cause of that fire that ripped across the Itradi countryside. Assuming, though, that the fire traveled in as even a radius as the evidence indicates, we're squarely in the middle here."

"So I'm going to do everything in my power to make sure we don't get annihilated by ancient magic fire," she went on, stepping closer. "Is that practical enough for you?"

In the time it took Darius to formulate a reply, Vasna heel-turned and snagged a surprised Maxos by the shoulder to light her way as she walked further in. The prince sighed and massaged his temples. He hadn't meant to offend her, nor had he expected her to take his impatience so personally. Whatever had gotten to her in here had really put her on edge. He made a note to choose his words more carefully for now as he followed behind at a distance.

"Hey, look there," Maxos said, pointing off into the distance. Darius squinted ahead and spotted the general's discovery. A violet glow pulsed in the distance. Their nearby light

169

sources had made it too hard to notice until now.

The three approached the glow cautiously. It came from huge stone disc set into the wall. Violet runes shined upon its surface, which extended up far into the darkness. Vasna signaled the Knights to stay put and stepped closer on her own, murmuring, "Don't touch it."

She looked the surface over for several seconds before making her assessment of it. "Looks like a door of some kind. These runes are in their language, that much I know. Unfortunately, my Itradi is more than a touch rusty, so I'm not going to get anywhere figuring this out unless I'm able to cast some spells, which means we run the risk of triggering some countermeasures."

"Best to take it slow then," Darius conceded, eager for a chance to side with Vasna. Perhaps she wouldn't hold his previous impatience against him.

He and Maxos stepped back to give Vasna plenty of room to work, but the calm moment they aimed to take was suddenly shattered by steady, deafening screech echoing through the halls. The Knights clapped their hands over their ears and turned back to Vasna who swore furiously. "Alarm ward!" she shouted over the piercing noise. "That was the first thing I looked for! How did I miss it?"

She began to dance her hands across the surface of the door, evoking a flash of golden light that silenced the alarm. The echo slowly faded away, but only to reveal rumbling footsteps pounding their way closer and closer.

"Keep working!" Darius shouted, as he and Maxos readied their weapons. "We'll cover you!" But that promise would be tough to keep. The same halls that had made the alarm seem to echo from every angle were also sounding back the footfalls of whatever approached. The two Knights stood back to back near Vasna, searching the darkness.

"There!" Maxos shouted. A split second later, a loud crash erupted from behind Darius, and he spun around to see one of the huge, undead warbeasts barreling toward them through the tables and devices, tossing them across the room as though they were toys.

Maxos was quick to leap high into the air to escape the charging beast, but the extra seconds Darius had taken to spin around were all that it had needed to catch him with its curved horns and knock him end-over-end backward into more old tables and shelves. The prince struggled to catch his breath from the impact that knocked the wind out of him.

He refocused on the beast as it barreled toward him, its empty eye sockets fixed on him and ragged wrappings trailing behind. Darius got his arm under a table and hurled it at the creature as he climbed to his feet, but it smashed through, undeterred by the impact. Once upright, the prince had but a moment to swing the Titangavel sideways, catching the warbeast in the side of its head and just barely diverting it from pinning him as it charged full tilt into the wall.

Had it been alive, Darius was certain that it would have knocked itself out upon slamming into the wall as hard as it did. Instead, the tireless beast rasped unnaturally from its empty throat and snapped at the prince, forcing him to leap backward to remain out of reach. The battle was beginning to remind Darius of the battle against the jinra in training. The unpleasant memory of being crushed drifted back into his mind.

Just as it looked as though it might charge him again, a salvo of shining bolts perforated its side. Maxos had dropped back out of the air on the other side of the room and now drew back his bowstring to let loose another spread.

The attack was stimulus enough to cause the warbeast to rear back up and charge his ally. This could be his chance. Darius wasn't as quick as Maxos was, but with the general diverting the

171

hulking creature, perhaps he could find an opening for his slower, more powerful blows. The headshot hadn't gotten him very far, so he'd have to try something else.

The prince broke into a sprint and caught up with the warbeast near its tree trunk-like hind legs, rearing back with the Titangavel, he loosed his second swing right into its kneecap with all of his might. The crunch of shattering bone confirmed that he'd done better this time, and the lower part of the creature's leg went limp, dangling sloppily.

The monster seemed to have no instinct as to how to compensate for its new, lopsided gait. It listed far to the right, missing Maxos before it collapsed onto its side.

"Finish it! Hurry!" Maxos cried, firing more shots into the prone beast's exposed chest. Each crackling bolt struck true, splintering its ribs.

"I can't rush this!" Vasna barked back from across the room.

The warbeast craned its neck toward the sound of Vasna's voice. Darius swore as it hefted itself back up on three legs and into motion, barreling toward Vasna.

He slung the Titangavel back over his shoulder and bolted after it, thankful that he and Maxos had managed to slow it by crippling a leg. His long strides carried him far enough ahead of the warbeast that he had time to face it and plant his feet. He spread his arms wide and leaned in as it plowed into him. He grasped its horns and held on with all of his might. The impact budged him several feet closer to Vasna, but soon he and the beast were locked into position, neither giving ground to the other.

The prince wrestled with the warbeast's head, managing to compensate for its thrashing and keep it still, but he would tire and it would not. He couldn't hold it like this forever.

"Darius!" Maxos called to him, skidding into position several yards away, facing the beast's side. "When I hit it, twist to your left as hard as you can!"

"Got it!" the prince grunted back. He didn't know what Maxos could be planning, but he'd give anything a shot to drop the monster.

Out of the corner of his eye, Darius could see Maxos drawing back on Watchward again, but instead of making a spread of arrows as he had many times before, the general had concentrated the force of several of his lightning arrows into one. The crackling bolt grew as thick as a man's arm, and quivered with barely contained power.

A moment later, the shot cut loose. Its bright flash blinded Darius as it struck the beast's haunch, letting loose an echoing thunderclap, and Darius wrenched to his left with all of his might. Though he couldn't see, he could feel the tension of the monster's body tilting the opposite direction of its head. A sickening ripping and shredding sound followed, and suddenly all of the pressure bearing down on Darius ceased.

He didn't need to be able to see to understand what had happened. Darius dropped the detached head to the ground with a dry thump and collapsed to his knees panting to wait for his strength and sight to return.

The tap of footsteps approached from where Maxos had fired. "You still in one piece?" The general asked, clearly winded as well.

Darius grunted an affirmative and put his hand out in the direction of Maxos' voice. "Good plan," he added.

"Good twist," the general replied with a chuckle, clasping the prince by the arm and hauling him to his feet.

Darius grinned, pleased to have the open approval of his more seasoned ally.

"I think I've got it," he heard Vasna call out as the last colorful blotches faded from his sight. She spoke a short phrase in what he suspected was Itradi. As she completed it, the glowing figures on the disc flashed once more before fading out, and the massive stone rolled aside to reveal a gaping natural cavern beyond. Dim light flickered deep within it, casting odd shadows on the uneven walls.

Maxos stepped up beside her and looked into the passage. "So, the door took some kind of command to open? What was it?"

Vasna bit her lower lip for a moment before she responded, "The phrase means, 'Though the Stars defy us, we endure.'"

All three of them shifted uncomfortably. The phrase had considerable gravity when spoken in the common tongue of Vatrisland. Vasna wouldn't have translated their words to say 'the Stars' so properly, as opposed to 'stars' or any particular star unless she'd taken their words to mean it in that very specific fashion. The word she'd used referred to the powers of the Aurora Arms. It meant that the writer was condemned by the very mystical aurora that the Knights revered.

Darius hustled up beside his two companions, resolved to lead by example. "I think we'd best get moving if that's the case," he said. "We're already at odds with that necromancer, and if he's hiding down here, he's probably after whatever the Itradi hid with those words. Let's get in there and stop him for good."

Maxos and Vasna nodded, and all three of them started forward.

Upon stepping up into the cavern, Vasna winced sharply. Darius looked back to see her pressing her lips tightly together. She looked almost ashamed on seeing him and Maxos look back.

"Something wrong?" Darius asked.

Vasna shook her head and stepped forward, but now she had an obvious limp.

"Whoa, what happened to your leg?" Darius pressed her.

At first she looked as though she might claim to be fine again, but instead she leaned against the wall and tugged a flap of her coat aside, showing her leg to the Knights.

Maxos just swore and turned away. Darius knelt down and looked closer, tugging a narrow hole in Vasna's right pant leg slightly wider to expose her skin to the light. Just above the top of her boot, a small black wound extended dark, slender tendrils across her skin in all directions.

"It happened when I slid down among the undead from the aqueduct," she said grimly. "One of those things just barely got a finger on me before you made it down. I didn't want to tell the two of you. It would have only slowed us down, or worse yet, you'd have insisted we turn back and try to treat it somehow."

Darius just stared numbly at the wound for a moment. He'd watched a normal soldier be drained to a blackened husk from several seconds held in the mummy's grip. He'd felt the pain of the black wound himself, but he'd had the power of the Titangavel to help him recover from it. Now, in a quiet moment instead of the chaos of battle, that blotch on Vasna's leg seemed like the most horrifying thing he'd ever seen.

Maxos turned back to face Vasna. "I suppose you wouldn't have hidden it from us if you knew that there was nothing to worry about?"

She shook her head. "If their touch doesn't kill you outright, even the smallest wound will still grow. It's going to spread up my leg and work its way toward my heart. When it gets there, well…." She trailed off and shrugged.

"Damn you, Darius," Maxos muttered angrily, turning away from both of them. "And damn me for following you. I knew this was a bad idea, but I let my loyalty to the Oracle and to the Knights guilt me into following you."

"No, no, no!" Darius stammered quickly as he sprung up to address the general. "We can fix this. I can fix this. All we have to do is get her back to Cloudbreach and we can give her one of the Aurora Arms. I've recovered from much worse with the Titangavel. All we have to do is get her home."

175

"So you're going to use up one of your three remaining weapons to save her life?" Maxos countered. "You're just going to make her an Aurora Knight to fix your mistake? You can't just do that, Darius! I want to save her too, but this isn't like your life as a prince where nothing's scarce. We only have five weapons."

Darius cringed. Maxos' argument made sense, but she'd come so far to help them. She didn't deserve to die, and they could do something about it. Surely she'd be better off as an Aurora Knight, even if it did mean facing further danger. "She's got the spirit for it. I think she'd make a great Knight!" he fired back.

"Hey!" Vasna interrupted them forcefully. "Full stop!"

The two Knights were stunned into silence. Vasna strode over to them red-faced in as fast and as dignified a manner as she could with her limp and hissed sternly, "Knock it off! Both of you!"

Darius and Maxos both started to argue, but Vasna refused to relinquish control, darting her eyes back and forth between the two of them as she went on. "No! Listen! While you two are standing here bickering over who's going to make me what, I've got cursed, black creepers crawling up my leg. I do not have the time, gentlemen. None of this matters if this thing kills me before we get back to Cloudbreach, so I want both of you to *shut up*."

She stopped briefly, looking at each of them in turn expectantly until they each nodded.

"Now we're going to keep moving. We're going to go down and find that necromancer, and when we find him, we are going to stop him. Then we find a way to get that glowing wall down and get Vatrisland's troops and ourselves out of here. Provided I'm still breathing after that, I leave my fate in your hands, but until then we will focus on the task at hand. Have I made myself perfectly clear?"

She didn't wait for them to respond. Instead, she heel-turned on her good leg and limped deeper into the cavern. Darius and Maxos looked at one another and exchanged defeated nods. They fell into step beside her as she made her way down the sloping passage.

17

The light at the end of the passageway grew brighter. The soft glow that the Aurora Arms had emitted in the darkness gradually faded as Darius' eyes adjusted to the flickering firelight coming from sconces up ahead. Their path ended onto a downward spiraling ledge that lined the inside of a broad vertical shaft.

The three stepped out to the edge of the chasm and looked to see how far down it extended. The sight that greeted them took Darius' breath away.

The shaft was not the empty expanse it had appeared to be during their approach. The view to the bottom was blocked by the massive, scaly green head of a creature whose suspended body extended perhaps a dozen stories downward. Its flared, cobra-like hood filled the width of the pit, making it even more broad and menacing. Wicked razor-sharp spines trailed down its back from the top of its head and a breeze rushed through the cavern at each of the creature's slow, shuddering breaths.

Vasna murmured in awe, "What is that thing?"

Darius and Maxos gaped silently. Just standing the creature's presence caused prince's stomach to churn. It seemed even more great and terrible for Vasna's inability to put a name or reason to it.

Maxos swallowed quietly. "Whatever it is, it seems to be asleep. Let's keep it that way, shall we?" he whispered.

The group crept down the spiraling walkway, taking care with each step as they studied more and more of the colossal creature. Huge jeweled hoops pierced its hood, and linked it to golden chains anchored to the walls. Another length of similar chains crisscrossed its body all the way down, binding a pair of muscular arms and two pairs of mighty legs to its body. Thick, bony plates protruded from great stretches of its skin, looking so sturdy that Darius questioned the ability of even the Titangavel to shatter them.

Darius made conversation to try to calm his nerves. "And I thought dragons were frightening," he said quietly.

"You've seen a dragon before?" Maxos questioned.

"Not up close," the prince had to admit. "I was out in one of the border towns on a hunting trip when it attacked. Even from a distance it was a sight. It ate men like a man eats a turkey. This guy," he added, pointing at the sleeping monstrosity, "could eat a dragon like that."

"Gentlemen," Vasna said, "if it's all the same to you, I'd prefer to not dwell on how edible I may or may not be." Her voice wavered slightly as she spoke. No doubt the pain of her wound was still gnawing at her. Darius dropped the issue.

In the silence that followed, Darius heard a hoarse voice echoing up the shaft. Maxos and Vasna seemed to catch it over the cyclical breaths of the nearby beast. All three crouched low, continuing down the walkway and staying behind occasional stone protrusions as they could find them.

Soon they were close enough to make out the words that the voice spoke.

"Hrax," the man's voice cooed like he was talking to a sleepy child, "I know you can hear me, great one. It is I, Zavian. Can you smell them, even in your sleep? I have brought an offering of souls for you. Thousands of soldiers wait for you above. They are trapped and ripe for devouring. Rise and feast, great one. I await your satisfaction, and your reward."

The creature hanging in the shaft, presumably Hrax,

breathed unevenly as if in response. The ground shuddered, and Vasna and the Knights braced themselves in their hiding place to avoid toppling. Maxos mouthed "Hrax?" to Vasna, but the captain shook her head and shrugged in response.

The necromancer had lured Vatrisland's forces out to sacrifice them to this beast. Darius swallowed yet more guilt. They'd never have come so far into the Cryptwastes with so many if they hadn't been emboldened by the Aurora Knights' presence. They had to stop this Zavian before he woke Hrax.

The prince peeked out over the side of the spire of rock they'd hidden behind. Zavian faced their direction from an altar at which he continued to cry out at the creature above. Darius quickly ducked back down. They couldn't risk an approach from the front. If the group could circle to the necromancer's blindside, they'd have a shot at dropping him in one attack. He signaled to the others with a hand gesture to go further downhill, and then to Maxos, pantomiming a bow and arrow firing motion. They nodded and kept moving.

Zavian continued beseeching Hrax. They were lucky this process was so involved. In a few moments they'd gotten out of the necromancer's peripheral vision. Now all they would have to do is stay quiet and make it around the next quarter of the room's edge. Darius tightened his grip on the Titangavel, wishing he could be the one to strike the blow, but with so much at stake, assurance was far more important than vindication.

Suddenly, Vasna gasped. Loudly.

They had no cover here. Maxos dropped to the ground, tugging her flat with him. Darius followed suit. Long moments stretched out. He didn't dare move a muscle. Their angle above Zavian would keep them out of sight. The noise could have easily been a whistle of Hrax's irregular breathing through a narrow gap between stones. It could be anything Zavian wanted it to be as long as he didn't expect intruders.

Zavian no longer called out to the beast above him. For a moment, the chamber quieted, save for Hrax's rhythmic breaths.

"So you've come," Zavian mused.

None of the three made a sound.

"You should know it's already too late," he continued with unsettling giddiness. "Hrax's sleep is deep, but Vatrisland's troops are close and plentiful. He smells them by now, and I assure you, he is salivating with anticipation."

Darius looked to Vasna, expecting to see her clutching her leg in pain. Why else would she have gasped so loudly? She lay flat on her belly, head raised just slightly, eyes transfixed on the necromancer.

No. The angle was wrong for that. It was something past the necromancer. Darius followed her gaze to the middle of the chamber, where an altar stood upon a raised dais.

A greatsword as long as the Titangavel and cast from metal as pale as winter snow rested on the altar. Though firelight from nearby braziers flickered wildly in Hrax's windy breaths, the blade reflected nothing. A round onyx set into the center of the hand guard was the only defining feature Darius could take in from his distance.

"If you really want to be audience to Hrax's awakening, you can remain where you are," the voice declared again. "I promise you, Aurora Knights, he will not disappoint."

Maxos took action. He rocked his upper body backward, shifting from his belly onto his knees and drawing Watchward's bowstring in one smooth motion. The bolt arced loose from the bow before he even finished his motion. So much for subtlety. Darius righted himself and bounded into the air to follow up.

The black-robed figure looked gaunt and sickly, but countered them with supernatural speed. In one motion, he went from first hurling a cluster of violet phantoms toward Maxos from a cobra-headed staff, to then thrusting the staff high. White bones, curved like a ribcage and as thick as tree trunks, burst forth from the ground, forming a shell between the necromancer and Darius.

Maxos' bolts struck the new obstacle, scattering their power harmlessly against it, followed by Darius. The new obstacle ruined the prince's swing and his hammer clattered noisily off of the wall at an odd angle.

"Rise, Hrax!" Zavian cried, his staff thrust skyward in one hand as he beckoned the beast with his other. Rumbling breaths from the hanging creature grew louder still. The tip of its tail began to wriggle from side to side.

Darius scrambled to his feet once more and hammered with the Titangavel against the bones that blocked his path, but they held fast. Undeterred, he lashed the weapon to his back and tried to squeeze between through the gaps, but his armor dug into his flesh painfully as he tried. His fingers and arms ached with effort as he tried to pry the ribs further apart. "Maxos," he yelled in desperation, "take the shot! Take it!"

But the shot didn't come. Darius turned his gaze upward to see the general streaking back and forth across the chamber as lightning. Every time he landed long enough to draw back on Watchward's bowstring, another cluster of screaming phantoms descended on him, forcing him back into motion.

Darius stepped back, trying to calm his frantic mind in the chaos. He wasn't out of options yet. He gripped the Titangavel once more and drew his arms apart slowly, focusing on the cavern floor beneath his feet.

Solid rock resisted his weapon's call more than dirt and clay did. The entire cavern groaned under the stress of Darius' command to open a fissure. Beads of sweat formed on his forehead as he strained and roared. Rocks from high above, freed as the cavern started to contort, crashed down, exploding as they landed. The prince struggled to keep his mind from wandering to thoughts about how many tons of earth and ancient ziggurat were between him and the surface, lest he lose his nerve.

The first crack formed in the floor like a shadowy streak of lightning zigzagging along the dark stone. Slowly it widened, further and further, wrenching a pair of the sturdy ribs apart. Zavian glanced frantically back and forth between Hrax and Darius, crying out to the great beast, "Hurry, Hrax! Rise!"

The beast's writhing quickened. There wasn't much time. Sweat stung Darius' eyes as he yelled and strained against the ancient rock. The bones quivered under the pressure until finally, with an echoing crack, two broke free from their anchor points. With the ribs yanked wide, he rocked the Titangavel into a ready position, bounded through the gap, and swung with everything he had squarely at Zavian's chest.

His blow didn't land.

In the split second before he could end the fight, the necromancer found another surge of inhuman speed. He brought his cobra-headed staff to bear on Darius and loosed a withering ray that buckled the prince. Darius' arms refused to bear the Titangavel cleanly to its target, and his knees gave out under his body weight. He toppled helplessly backward, landing on the concave side of one of the nearby ribs.

"I have come too far to see you ruin this for me, Aurora Knight," Zavian hissed, keeping the beam from his staff aimed at the prince. "You would seek to rob me of life on the very day Hrax promises me freedom from this mortal burden? I will not have it!"

Darius writhed and growled. Every inch of his skin crawled with excruciating pain. His muscles refused any command he gave them, instead quivering violently. He could feel his teeth clenching so hard that they might crack.

Consciousness began to slip away. He had failed them all. Maxos and Vasna. Vatrisland's troops. His father. The Oracle. The world. They would all be left at the mercy of the colossal monster awakening above him.

183

Suddenly, a flash of light rocked the staff hard to one side. Darius' vision began to clear with the beam no longer focused on him. As his senses and strength started to return, he spotted the staff. Whatever had struck it had ripped it free from the necromancer's hands, knocked it through a gap in the bone wall, and sent it clattering across the chamber. Without his staff to suppress the prince, Zavian's eyes went wide.

"Darius!" Vasna cried in the distance. "Darius, finish him!"

Darius quickly regained muscle control and looked to one side, searching in the direction of the voice. Above him, peeking over the side from a higher point on that spiraling walkway, lay Captain Hain with her magelock pistol still fixed and pointing toward where the staff had been.

"Get up, Darius! Get up!" she shouted at him again.

Though his muscles still quivered with exhaustion, he pushed himself to his knees. Zavian stood before him shaking, still looking back and forth between him and Hrax as he made more shrill cries to the beast to awaken. Above, Hrax's writhing grew more pronounced. The massive enchanted chains binding the great creature groaned against its stirring. Darius willed himself to his feet. He could feel the Titangavel's power returning his strength to him, but in his mind he begged the weapon to work faster still.

"This ends here, you bastard!" Darius cried, gripping the Titangavel so hard that his arms shook. He wound the weapon back, stepped forward, and slammed its head into Zavian's chest with everything he had.

Whatever had given the necromancer the speed and magical power with which he'd fought the Knights and commanded the undead hordes, had not made him any sturdier than a mortal man. The crushing blow knocked Zavian off his feet, tumbling backward, and into the wall that had protected him. His crumpled form slid down the curved bone surface, landing in a heap on the ground, unmoving.

All Darius wanted to do was collapse in exhaustion, but the clatter and rumble above continued. He looked up. All he could manage to do was murmur, "No. No, no."

Hrax had not stopped awakening. The great beast thrashed left and right above him, now letting out breathy, ringing screams. It strained with its six limbs against the chains that held it, and the sounds of shearing metal that echoed throughout the chamber made clear that it would soon be free. Darius stood, stunned at the sight.

More shouts from Vasna broke through the cloud of despair that had come over him. She was calling his name. He looked up to see her cradled in Maxos' arms on the walkway. "Darius! Grab the sword and get up here! Hurry!"

The prince looked back at the altar. The pale blade that had distressed Vasna and given their presence away lay before him. Something about it deeply unsettled him, but Vasna seemed absolutely emphatic that he bring it up.

He could question her about it later. He slung the Titangavel over his shoulder by its strap and grabbed the great sword before bounding up from ledge to ledge to join his friends.

"Good, good," Vasna slurred breathlessly. "So much power. We have to know what it is. Can't just let it stay."

"Heads up!" Maxos warned him. The Knights lunged backward. Another boulder that had broken free from above crashed down, taking a chunk out of the ledge where they'd stood a moment earlier.

Darius and Maxos looked up once more, in time to see Hrax shatter the chains that had held him in place. Huge golden links rained down the shaft, clanging deafeningly on the floor as they landed. The beast spread its newly freed arms and legs wide, making it appear even larger and more terrible still. It found purchase against the spiral walkway with its four legs, and reached up with its hands, easily ripping loose the chains binding its pierced hood to the wall.

Now completely free, Hrax lashed out violently. The Knights dodged frantically as it hefted its massive body further up the shaft and began to burrow through the solid rock ceiling as easily as a man digs through sand.

"Up, up, up!" Maxos yelled, sprinting around the spiraling walkway with Vasna still cradled to his chest. Darius kept up with the mysterious sword in hand, grateful once more for the strength of the Aurora Arms. He didn't want to imagine how far back they'd be if either needed to carry Vasna under his own ordinary strength.

A great cloud of dust began to billow up from the debris striking the floor of the chamber. It raced upward quickly, threatening to overtake them as they ran. Dodging falling rocks would be considerably harder without clear vision. Darius and Maxos poured on an extra measure of speed as they neared the top of the spiral, rounding the last corner and bringing the passageway out of the chamber into view.

Then that massive tail whipped around toward the trio, carving through stone like a farmer's scythe slashed through stalks. Each Knight threw himself the ground, narrowly avoiding the crushing appendage as it passed overhead. The rocks it had dislodged battered each of them in a wake behind the tail. Darius looked ahead, squinting to keep anything from striking his eyes. Maxos had thrown himself on Vasna, guarding her from the worst of it. Now he groaned and strained to shake the debris off of them.

"Hold up! I've got you!" Darius called, racing to his friends. He hefted the rubble off of Maxos and pulled him to his feet. "You okay?"

"Yeah, yeah," Maxos replied. The general was still focused on the task at hand. He knelt down to scoop Vasna back up and grunted in pain.

Darius narrowed his eyes. "Stars, he got you good, didn't

186

he?"

"Boys," Vasna interrupted them, "that's not the only problem."

The Knights turned their attention to where she was pointing. She wasn't kidding. Hrax's lashing tail had collapsed the tunnel from which they had come into the chamber. Now, a wall of rubble stood between them and their way out.

Darius glanced back and forth between the blocked passage and the rising dust cloud. There was no time for him to pound or dig his way through that rubble. All the while, the hulking beast clawed its way further and further upward, raining down more chunks of the cavern ceiling. They needed a new plan, but a quick glance around the chamber didn't reveal any options.

Then a flicker of light caught the prince's eye. He looked up where Hrax continued clawing away at the ceiling and hissing, eager to find the light's source.

Another flicker. This time he had his eyes fixed upward.

It was sunlight. Hrax had found the surface. If they followed the beast, they could get out. If they could get out, they could fight it.

"We're going up. Maxos, swap with me," Darius commanded suddenly, passing the white sword to the general and scooping up Vasna.

"Up?" Maxos questioned. He followed Darius' gaze to the ceiling and understood. "Guess that is our best shot." He secured the sword to himself and tried to flex out the pain from the rocks that had struck him.

Vasna clung tightly to Darius as he kept his eyes on Hrax. Together, they watched for an opportunity to make their move. "I'll go first and you follow," the prince murmured to Maxos. The general nodded in agreement.

At last, that great, destructive tail sucked upward through the gap and bright sunlight streamed into the chasm. Chunks of the newly carved tunnel were still falling, but the passage wouldn't get any more stable before they had to go. Darius coiled his leg muscles and steeled his will.

"Now!" He bounded into the air, racing upward into the vertical shaft. With Vasna occupying his arms, he'd have to rebound off of the walls of the pit to keep finding new contact points. He wouldn't have many opportunities to change direction on the way out. He'd have to make the few he'd get count.

His feet touched the first wall and he coiled his legs in response. With only a moment, he craned his neck to look up into the chaotic mess of dancing light and shadows. Shadows were bad. Shadows meant rocks. He picked the biggest gap of light he could judge and shoved off again. The Titangavel's blessing didn't disappoint. His body obeyed his commands with precision and split-second reactions.

Look. Leap. Look. Leap. Flying pebbles scraped his face. Larger rocks struck his armor noisily, threatening to knock him off balance. The shaft grew brighter, but he didn't dare lose focus. He wondered how Maxos was doing beneath him, but he couldn't risk a look downward to check.

The final rebound came. With one last elated push, Darius hurled himself and Vasna into the sunlight. He skidded to a stop on the capital streets, clutching her tightly. He'd been so focused on his efforts that he hadn't registered her screams all the way up until now. He laid the trembling captain down to let her recover on solid ground. "We got it! We made it." He repeated himself a few times to reassure her.

A thunderclap and a bright flash heralded Maxos successful exit. He came out of the crackling light and tumbled sloppily to a stop on the ground, groaning in pain. He'd be better soon thanks to Watchward. The important part was that they'd escaped the cavern.

With his allies safe, Darius took a moment to assess their

situation. Undead wandered about in the distance, but without Zavian's governance, they seemed directionless. The city had been devastated even more so now than for what he'd done to it. Hrax's exit made the prince's quake look laughable by comparison. A broad path of shambles stretched on for over a mile.

And at the end of the path, Hrax towered at his full height. His long strides covered dozens of yards each, carrying him further and further toward the southern horizon. Even from such a great distance, his screeching hisses forced Darius to cover his ears.

The prince scowled, dismayed. Chasing the beast was out of the question right now. Even at top speed, their hounds would never keep up. Even if they could, what would he do? Until he assembled all of his Knights, he'd have no hope of stopping something so powerful.

Reluctantly, Darius put thoughts of pursuit behind him and turned back to his friends. In the moments that he'd been watching Hrax, Vasna had pulled up her pant leg and had taken up assessing her wound. The prince grimaced. In the few hours since she'd been hit, her wound had grown to the size of his hand. Its black spidery veins reached past her knee. She looked as though her earlier bravery about it had left her, and now there was a numbness and emptiness about her as she stared at it.

Seconds later, she caught him looking at it and quickly tugged the pant leg back down. Her face flushed. She cleared her throat and told him, "You should see if you can talk to the Oracle. She'll be able to call The Relentless and point them toward us."

Darius shook his head to clear his own worries about her. "Right, yeah." He gripped the Titangavel and called out to the Oracle.

"Darius? Yes, I'm here!" her voice replied in his head. It was the first truly comforting thing he'd heard in several days.

"Oracle, something got free from beneath the ziggurat. The necromancer called it 'Hrax.' Have your maidens warn Fort

Diligence that it's headed their way."

"We were afraid of that," she replied grimly.

"What is it? What do you know about it?"

"He's an insatiable, ruinous beast from another reality. What he was doing beneath Anceda Pryta, I can't imagine, but we're neck deep in history here learning what we can. I wish I could say that I had something more for you, but our resources are a bit divided at the moment."

"Divided?" Darius asked.

She didn't respond for several seconds.

"Darius," she began tentatively, "your father has declared that he plans to occupy Aurora Tower."

"What? On what grounds?"

"He says that there is a spy among our shrine maidens; someone trying to undermine Vatrisland. It's just an excuse to embed his soldiers in the tower."

"You sound pretty sure about that, Oracle. He has a responsibility to protect Vatrisland, though. If you're wrong about this, you could be harboring an enemy of the kingdom."

"I'm not wrong on this, Darius. I...I just know that he has another motive," she murmured hesitantly.

Something was off. Darius furrowed his brow. "How do you know?" She didn't answer. "There's something you're not telling me."

"Darius," she began firmly, "it's my duty to protect the Knights and the Arms from anything that might divert them from the task of protecting the world. I cannot give anyone the benefit of the doubt when it comes to that task, and that includes your father. Someday, you'll understand why I have to refuse."

Darius rubbed a hand over his face in frustration. "Oracle, that's not going to go well. My father's not going to just shrug and take it if you tell him no."

"I know," she answered flatly.

He sighed. A fight between his father and the Oracle would only weaken and distract both of them. If they were both going to be this stubborn, he needed to get home quickly. Maybe he could talk some sense into the two of them before things got completely out of hand.

He moved over beside Vasna, got under her arm, and helped her to her feet. "Look, Vasna's injured, so we need to come back to Cloudbreach anyway. Let me get there and talk to my father and we'll figure this out. Is The Relentless up and running?"

"One of my maidens just finished talking to Treve," the Oracle answered. "He says they can get airborne, but full speed is out of the question."

"Okay. Tell them to fly west until they hit Fort Bulwark, then as the crow flies toward Anceda Pryta. That should keep them from running into Hrax. We'll ride along the same path to meet up with them as quickly as we can."

"Understood. Be careful, Darius."

"Yeah, you too," he murmured.

Darius scooped Vasna into his arms so he could hustle faster than she could limp. Maxos got to his feet and fell into step beside him and they set out toward the basement in which they'd hidden their hounds.

18

In what Darius could only consider to be a stroke of incredible luck, Hrax's exit failed to do any additional damage to the structure in which they had hidden their riding hounds. He slid down into the lower chamber to find them excitedly straining against the pillar to which they'd been hitched. A few minutes of feeding and reassuring head scratches calmed the dogs enough that he and his allies could lead them safely out of the pit.

The sun had begun to set in the western sky, casting an orange light over the ruined city. The fiery glow only served to make the whole scene more hellish and surreal as they climbed onto their mounts and rode out.

Once they were on the move, Maxos rode up alongside the prince. "Darius, I need a word with you."

Darius looked back. Vasna was following far enough behind to be out of earshot. He turned his attention back to the general to find him stone-faced and serious. "What is it, Maxos?"

Maxos looked away for a moment. He seemed uncomfortable, as if he were torn between speaking and staying silent. "First thing's first," he began, quickly pushing the pale sword they'd taken out of the cavern into Darius' arms. "I'm not following you to meet up with The Relentless, so you better take this back to Cloudbreach with you."

Darius accepted the weapon, nearly fumbling it in the sudden transfer. He looked down at it, then back at the general. "What? Why not?" he asked.

"No doubt Hrax is headed toward Fort Diligence to collect on Zavian's promised sacrifice," Maxos explained. "I can't do much about that part, but once he's done there, where do you think he'll head next?"

Darius shrugged as he quickly secured the sword to his own mount. "Who knows? I don't think we can make any reasonable guesses about it."

"Think, Darius." Irritation crept into Maxos' voice. "Zavian motivated Hrax to awaken by offering him souls. Once he's done with the fort, where's the next nearest ready supply of tons of people?"

His question put everything together. "The H'tyanni capital. So you're headed to Aksa'ol then," the prince stated, looking ahead and nodding. "Won't your superiors want to touch base with you?"

Maxos shrugged. "Too bad for them," he said, unpinning his rank insignia and holding it out to Darius. "If you run into them, you can tell them where I went. They're welcome to come find me if they want to question my decision."

Darius took the shining pins in his hand and looked down at them. "Maxos, this is a lot to just give up. Are you sure you want to do this?"

The general shook his head, pressing his lips together firmly before answering, "Stars, Darius, you still don't get it do you?"

"What's your problem, Maxos?" Darius countered. "I'm trying to figure you out, but all you're giving me is bitter attitude. Where's the man I met a few days ago at the fort?"

"The man you met a few days ago was trying very, very hard to make the best of a bad situation," Maxos growled. "Unfortunately for him, since then you've made one hasty call after another. You led a charge that got good soldiers trapped in the wastes. You brought Vasna out into a dangerous situation, and now her life's in danger."

"We needed her!" Darius interrupted defensively. He glanced back at Vasna to see her furrowing her brow, but she kept her distance. The prince lowered his voice. "She got us into that chamber and she saved my life. Don't forget that we killed Zavian today, either."

"At the cost of thousands of Vatrisland's soldiers and potentially one of the finest minds in the whole nation," he said, gesturing to Vasna. "And on top that we have the most wildly destructive abomination I've ever seen roaming the world's surface. That's a disappointing debriefing to say the least."

"Okay," Darius growled, "you've got me. I'm blowing this Knight-Captain thing. Happy? I mean, we can fixate on it, or we can keep moving and keep trying to do something about it. I haven't been doing this as long as you have. I'm still figuring it out."

"Exactly." Maxos pounced on his last line, shaking a finger at him sharply to punctuate his point. "We wouldn't be cleaning up all of these messes if we'd had someone experienced leading the Knights like the Oracle had originally planned. But then she tells me a few days ago that she's had to make some 'political concessions' to get the Aurora Arms out."

"Wait a minute," Darius shot back. "You were in touch with the Oracle before I came out here?"

"I was supposed to be the Knight-Captain, Darius!"

Silence fell over both of them. Darius' mouth hung slack. He looked at Vasna, who'd opened her mouth as though she'd been about to cut in, but closed it again in the awkward silence. All Darius could manage on looking back at the scowling, glaring Maxos was, "What?"

"You displaced me, Darius." His tone had softened to more disappointment than anything. "I've known I was meant to be the Knight-Captain for four years. I prepared for it. I chose Knights, and then you, in your privilege, get the position handed over to you on a platter. Hardly a damn day of real experience, and here you are."

Darius couldn't bring himself to speak, so Maxos continued, "So if I seem bitter, or like I take this Aurora Knight business too seriously, it's because I've had a long, long time to think about it."

The prince's heart sunk. He'd barely thought about who should have been the Knight-Captain, and these past few days, the man had been fighting by his side. Maxos had bottled up his disappointment for the sake of the world. He'd endured Darius' failures and followed his lead, no doubt thinking all along about how he'd have done things if he'd been in charge. No wonder the general had gotten so short-tempered. Darius had robbed him.

"Maxos, I..." Darius began. "I'm sorry." He offered his apology with sincerity, but he knew it fixed nothing. Every failure he'd faced so far as an Aurora Knight had been something he thought he could correct if he just tried again or tried harder. This was different. The Titangavel, as well as the right of leadership that it carried, had been bound to him. This couldn't be undone.

"Save it," Maxos muttered, exasperated. "I know it's selfish of me to bring it up, but there it is. Now you know."

The general motioned to Vasna and she finally rode forward to join them. "I'm sorry for what I said earlier. Because you weren't a soldier, I didn't think you'd have what it took to be a Knight, but you're like Goso. If you decide to accept one of the weapons from Darius, I want you to know, I'll be honored to fight beside you."

"Like Goso?" she asked, cocking her head.

"Sorry," Maxos clarified. "Goso of the Danma. He's the wolverine; the spirit of unstoppable resolve. You're blessed by him, I'm sure."

Vasna nodded. "Thank you, General," she told him

195

somberly. "That means a lot to me."

The general returned her a quick nod of his own. "And I take it you're going to gather the rest of the Aurora Arms?" he asked Darius, focused and professional once more. "It looks like you're going to have to find the rest of your candidates in the field. We can't hope to defeat Hrax until we're all assembled. Until then, we have to just do the best we can to keep the world safe."

Darius cleared his throat. "I…I think that sounds good," he replied timidly. He couldn't seem to switch back to business-as-usual so quickly like Maxos just had. He still dwelt on his inability to make up for what he'd taken from the general. "Hey, Maxos, look. You said you chose your Knights a while ago. I know it doesn't fix this, but I'd be more than willing to take your choices into consideration."

Maxos hesitated for a moment, looking into the dark eastern sky. Darius squirmed slightly. His armor clanked conspicuously over their hounds' quiet, steady trot.

"One of my chosen lives in Aksa'ol. If you get the Arms and hurry to join me, we'll have another good Knight at our side. To be honest, I think you'll find that you and she have a lot in common."

The heavy lump forming in Darius' stomach lightened a little. "I'll go back to Aurora Tower then, and gather the remaining Arms. If Hrax behaves like you think he will, then I'll meet up with you in Aksa'ol."

"We'll plan on that," the general confirmed with a stoic nod. "I'll keep in touch. The Danma watch over you." With that, he turned his hound to the southeast, spurred it into a speedy lope, and began riding for the H'tyanni border.

Darius watched the general ride into the distance for several seconds before he shook his head and refocused on the task at hand. "How's the leg?" he asked Vasna.

"Believe me," she said, shaking her head, "you don't want

to know. And the magic radiating from that sword you're carrying isn't making things any better. Let's just keep going. I'll do what I can to power through it."

"Right," Darius replied. He and Vasna spurred their hounds and headed southwest toward Fort Bulwark to meet their ride home.

XXX

Darius and Vasna rode on into the night. Their hounds, in their natural loyalty and eagerness to please, pressed on through growing exhaustion. Though their steps grew clumsy as the moon passed overhead, but they didn't let up or whimper any complaints.

Vasna didn't complain either, but it was clear to Darius that the pain had grown worse. The moonlight glittered through tears clinging to her cheeks, and she clenched her teeth tightly at each bounce and jostle.

Every mile they covered on their own would be one more that The Relentless wouldn't have to fly to meet up with them, but Darius grimaced watching Vasna suffer. He knew that time was only making her wound worse, but he wanted badly to stop, even for a moment, to ease her pain.

"We should feed and water the hounds. I can feel this boy getting tired," he told her. It was true, but he mostly offered it to save her the shame of asking for rest. He suspected she'd let her body break before her pride.

Vasna hesitated briefly before agreeing. They pulled their hounds to a stop and Darius dismounted. Though the day had been exhausting, he found himself less thirsty than he thought he should be. Maybe the Titangavel gave him the endurance to press on longer without sustenance alongside its other blessings. He was relieved regardless. The less water he needed, the more he could share with the dogs.

"Do you want me to help you out of your saddle?" he offered Vasna. "I'm feeling pretty sore myself."

She shook her head. "The less I move the better," she replied between sips from her canteen. When she finished, she leaned forward and rested her head on the soft furry neck of her hound, gently stroking and scratching the dog's throat as she rested.

Darius dug a pouch of dried meat from his pack and set to work caring for the grateful hounds. The break seemed as good a time as any to address a question that had nagged at him since Maxos had left them. "Maxos spoke as though you might refuse to accept one of the Aurora Arms," he began.

She didn't reply. She barely moved, save for one arm continuing to stroke the hound's neck.

"Do you think there's another way to fix this?" he asked her.

She answered flatly, "No."

Darius offered another large portion of dry meat to his hound. While the beast chewed noisily, he poured some water into a shallow dish on the ground. "So why wouldn't you take it?"

"I can't ask for that just to save my own life, Darius," she explained, her voice quivering slightly. "There are only five weapons. You can't just go handing one out because I got in over my fool head. You need to choose the right warriors for these."

He stepped over to Vasna's dog with the meat. The hound fought to dig its nose into the bag, slobbering hungrily. Darius took a minute to calm the beast before he served it. The task gave him time to think over Vasna's objection. "What if I think you're one of the right warriors?"

She'd had her head facing away from Darius, but now she picked it up and rested her opposite cheek on the dog so that she looked at him. A few more tears trickled down the side of her face, but she kept her voice composed. "Are you saying you would have chosen me even if I didn't need the weapon to save my life?"

Darius thought about it for a few moments before answering. "Honestly? I don't know."

She looked away again. "See?"

"See what?" he countered.

"You're just doing this to save me from my accident. You can't risk getting a bad Knight just to save my life. You owe the world better than that."

Darius sighed and thought hard, pretending to be lost in his focus on caring for the dogs. He wasn't ready to give this up. He needed to make her see this differently. After all, he honestly did think she'd make a great Knight.

He'd almost resigned himself to her decision when the answer came to him. He knew he had it, because he immediately felt peace, comforting and true.

"Vasna?"

"What?"

"I wouldn't have wanted to make you a Knight if you hadn't gotten that wound," he told her.

She looked at him once again, this time with her brow furrowed. He must have said it too enthusiastically, but he enjoyed her rare moment of confusion before he cracked the slightest smile.

"I wouldn't have chosen you because I'd never have had a chance to see the best of you," he explained sincerely.

"Oh, stars," she groaned, looking away once more.

The prince pressed on. "I'm serious. When you first got wounded, you refused to tell us about it, because you knew it would only distract us from the mission. When we eventually found out, you insisted that we push on so that you could help us as much as possible before the pain got to be too much for you. Even now, as you're insisting to me that you don't deserve to bear one of the Aurora Arms, you're proving yourself even more worthy. You're proving that you're ready to die to do what's best

199

for the world."

He circled around to the other side of the hound in hopes of making eye contact with her. She'd buried her face in the beast's neck. "Even if all of that means nothing to you," Darius went on, "you've got one of the finest heads for magic in the whole kingdom. This mission alone has proven that we're really going to need someone who knows the ins and outs of that stuff."

She still said nothing. Save for the riding hounds licking their chops in satisfaction, the lifeless Cryptwastes offered no sound to break the silence between them.

"Vasna," Darius urged her, "become an Aurora Knight."

She finally lifted her head. Though it was clear she was fighting pain, she somehow smiled through it as she fired back at him. "Well I can't very well say no if you're going to put on a display like that, can I?"

Darius grinned. "I meant every word."

She rolled her eyes and sat back upright. "Well don't waste them," she warned him. "I still need to get home in one piece or all of your sappy sentiment doesn't mean a thing."

"Right," Darius agreed, his spirits lifted. He hustled to put away all of the supplies he'd used to care for the hounds, both of which seemed to pick up on the renewed energy of their riders. In moments, they were back in motion.

19

With the first rays of morning sunlight streaming into her window, Ria gave up on getting any more sleep. What little she'd managed to get between long stretches of racing thoughts would have to do.

At least it hadn't been all for nothing. She'd decided how she would respond to Magnus today, and she was resolved to follow through.

She summoned Charise and sent her to wake the rest of the maidens with the message that she would be making an address in an hour. With the time she had left to herself, she dressed in her formal vestments and took extra care setting her hair just how she liked it.

If she was going to defy a king today, she was going to look the very picture of confidence and dignity while doing it.

Once she was satisfied, she exited her room to find the tower bustling. Most of the maidens, save for the ones who prepared breakfast, weren't used to waking this early. Many combed and tied their hair or ate their breakfasts as they walked to save time. She heard no complaints, though. Either they'd adjusted to the tense atmosphere over the past few days, or they didn't express their concerns within her earshot.

She made her way down to the second floor of the tower and proceeded to the front of the audience chamber where she seated herself and waited for everyone to arrive. In pairs and trios, the women made their way in and found seats. Nearly all of the groups murmured questions about what such an early audience could be for.

The tap of footsteps nearby tugged Ria's attention away from her casual eavesdropping. Charise arrived and knelt beside her. "I just took a look out of one of the front windows, Miss Ria. There's a lot of activity at the castle this morning. Guard activity, I mean. Seems like we don't have too much time."

Ria nodded. "Thank you, Charise. For everything." She smiled at the girl who had helped her so much lately before adding, "You know that, until the very last moment, you still have the same offer I'm about to extend to them."

Charise shook her head. "I'm not going anywhere, Oracle. Whatever happens after today, you can count on me to face it with you."

Ria fought the urge to tug the girl into a tight hug, instead just squeezing her on the shoulder. Though her offer was completely sincere, she wasn't sure what she would have done had Charise taken her up on it. The girl's declaration of loyalty calmed her.

The Oracle turned back to the crowd. Almost every seat was filled. She urged her aide to go find a seat of her own before rising and approaching the podium. The crowd of anxious girls and women quieted quickly, and gave her their full attention.

Though Ria had planned some of what she intended to say in advance, seeing all of her maidens seated before her stopped her short. Instead of sticking to the business-like opening that she'd planned, she looked away from her notes and took in the crowd.

"I want you to know how proud I am of all of you," she began. "This tower, this shrine, has gone decades without being thrown into high alert; without having Knights to look after. For each and every one of you, this is your first experience supporting an active team of Knights, and you have dazzled me with your creativity, your commitment, and your energy. You have adapted to the challenges before you, and have earned my highest admiration."

Some in the crowd beamed back at her, but many more still looked on with stilled expressions. Of course she wouldn't have called such an early gathering just to pat them on the back. She owed it to them to get to the point.

"As your Oracle, it falls upon me to speak for everyone who resides in this tower. It's a responsibility that I do not take lightly. You've put your lives and your safety into my hands, just as the Knights and people the world over put their lives and safety into ours.

"At the same time, I must also act in a way that will preserve the Aurora Arms, and the traditions of the Aurora Knights for future generations. Were the powers of the Arms ever subverted to put one man's needs or one kingdom's needs over all others, the grim tyranny that would follow would be more ruinous than the work of any monster.

"I'm sure all of you know by now that King Magnus has declared that he intends to have his soldiers occupy Aurora Tower. He takes action under the pretense of protecting his kingdom and his interests, but what he does today as an emergency measure will cede independence that we will almost certainly never recover."

She could feel the weight of her words beginning to settle over the room. None of the maidens made a sound.

"Vatrisland has been our adopted homeland since the Knights' inception, but we do not favor it over any other nation. You know well that your sisters come from all across the continent and beyond. If we allow any organization or government to insinuate itself into these halls, we will lose the neutrality that lets us act for the greatest good.

"Today, in order to protect our freedom, I will deny King Magnus' soldiers access to Aurora Tower. Furthermore, in the event King Magnus chooses to not respect this decision, we will respond by sealing our gates and activating this tower's protective wards."

An uneasy murmur passed through the crowd, but Ria continued. "I know that this decision distresses some of you. After all, a number of you come from Vatrisland. I myself call this nation my home. You may be thinking to yourself that this is not the mission for which you became a shrine maiden. Perhaps the thought of so openly defying a kingdom burdens your conscience.

"That's the very reason that I called you here at this hour; to offer you the opportunity to walk away with a clear conscience. I have no intention of dragging you along on a course of action that might alienate you from your family and friends, but if you wish to leave, you must decide and pack quickly. If I am forced to activate the tower's wards, there may be long stretches of time during which we cannot safely open the gates.

"But if you do stay here, you will be working to forge a new dawn for the Aurora Knights. Your efforts will carry us into a future in which we will not have to watch our backs or fear the pressures of manipulative politics. A future in which we are free. I hope you'll choose to be a part of that future. I leave the decision in your hands. You are dismissed."

Ria stepped away from the podium in silence as the maidens rose from their seats and began to talk amongst themselves. Charise rose to meet her when she reached the chairs where she'd left her. "How many do you think will take you up on your offer, Miss Ria?" the girl asked.

Ria sighed. She waved Charise to her side and walked toward an exit as she answered. "There will be some, no doubt, but we'll endure. What's important is that those who choose to stay will know that I didn't shackle them to my decision. So much of our mission is black and white. Nobody second guesses whether or not to fight against something like Hrax. This is different. This is the war of ideas. It's grey and messy. A maiden who walks away today may very well love both Vatrisland and the Aurora Knights. She isn't an enemy. She's just a woman who decided that the price of this fight was too high."

Charise nodded thoughtfully. "True. What about those of us who are staying? What should we be doing next?"

"For now, go see if any of your friends are preparing to leave," Ria told her. "If they are, they'll surely need help getting their things together in time. Magnus expects to bring his soldiers over within a few hours. I'll state our position and see if he chooses to respect us."

The two came to a stop near a window that looked out upon the castle. From the vantage point, Ria could see soldiers accumulating nearby. "If he refuses," she added, "we'll all be getting very familiar with the inside of this tower in the months to come."

XXX

The hours before Magnus' soldiers were expected to arrive flew by all too fast. Ria spent the majority of the time watching maidens come and go from a balcony a few floors above Aurora Tower's entrance. As she'd suspected, some number of her women had chosen to leave in response to her earlier speech. She counted no fewer than twenty tearful goodbyes between friends just outside of the tower's huge doors. She made a point to step out of view in those instances. Had she been a junior maiden trying to leave, she could easily imagine being with guilt seeing her Oracle standing watch as she left.

Soon after the last straggling maidens made their way out of the tower, King Magnus and the soldiers made their approach. The group wasn't very large, consisting of maybe two dozen lightly armored men in total. They marched in time across the expanse between the castle and the tower until they came to a halt just outside of the closed tower doors.

King Magnus, dressed in his royal robes, eyed Ria from the ground. "Good afternoon, Oracle," he called out. "I was hoping to meet with you eye-to-eye today to formalize our cooperation."

The gentle sincerity and practiced smile turned Ria's stomach instantly. Had she not already known who he really was, she knew she would have believed it. She did her best to keep her bitterness out of her tone as she replied. "I'm afraid I'm not familiar with the cooperation you're referring to, Your Majesty. Cooperation does not begin with a royal mandate."

"These are desperate times, Oracle," he explained in a patronizing coo. "The longer we delay on this matter, the more damage a spy could do to both my kingdom and your tradition."

"And if you don't find a spy, what then? How long would you investigate Aurora Tower if your search turned up nothing?" she challenged him, tucking her hands behind her back.

"Are you saying that you're certain none of your maidens have been compromised?"

Yes, she was. She wished for a moment that she could say it straight to his face. She wished that she could reveal exactly what Charise had overheard about planted evidence and dead, innocent pilgrims and rub it all in his pompous face. Too bad she couldn't afford to look like the very antagonist he'd invented to instigate his intrusion in the first place.

"If there is a spy, Your Majesty, we will ferret out the traitor on our own," she countered with steady confidence. "I have assigned some of my own to look into the claims you made yesterday. They are as educated and perceptive as any investigator you could send from the castle."

"So because you have maidens working on this, you deny assistance? Surely we could make faster progress if—"

"I deny invasion," Ria spat back, no longer able to contain her bitterness. "Enough games, Your Majesty. The action you propose to take is a wild overreach of your office. It violates the word and spirit of the agreement our predecessors made a thousand years ago. Though this tower stands on your castle grounds, it is and shall remain independent from all outer interference."

At that, the king lowered his voice. "Oracle, I cannot stand idly by while you harbor a fugitive. My soldiers must be allowed to search for threats to my kingdom, especially if those threats are as close to my home as your tower is."

"And if they are not?"

The king held a frozen scowl for a few moments. Ria wrapped her fingers tightly around her staff, daring him to say one threatening word with her glare. With no more than a gesture, she'd supercharge every ward on the tower to blast anyone who so much as spit on its outer walls.

Then, so abruptly that it made Ria jump, he burst into a loud fit of laughter.

"Well what do you expect me to say, Oracle? That I'll force the door? That I'll roll out the catapults and knock Aurora Tower to the ground? We both know that would be as good as declaring war on the whole continent, and that's not even considering that I'd be at war with the Aurora Knights, captained by my own son."

Ria stood at the edge of the balcony, gaping and speechless at the scene unfolding below her. The soldiers looked only slightly less bewildered by it all than she was.

"No, no, no," a red-faced Magnus went on, "I won't be doing anything of the sort." Then, with more composure he added, "But, naturally, you and your maidens can't expect to walk through my castle or on its grounds anymore without an escort. And I wouldn't expect any deliveries to arrive for the tower in a timely fashion from here on. After all, we'll need to thoroughly investigate anything going into or out of Aurora Tower to make certain that no one is sending aid to the spy. I'll just have to limit my pursuit of this spy to actions that don't 'wildly overreach my office,' as you say."

Ria refused to give him the satisfaction of making a facial expression, but inside, she boiled.

"Come along, then," he called, gesturing to the soldiers, who turned about-face and began marching back toward the castle.

Ria watched them leave. Instead of locking Magnus out, she and her maidens had effectively been locked in. Though the result was ultimately the same, it somehow tasted more like defeat.

When the crowd passed back into the castle, she turned and reentered the tower. Charise was there waiting for her, but didn't say a word. Ria strode past her briskly, barking, "Come." The girl fell into step.

"I want you to notify the kitchen that we're moving to an seventy percent ration. That ought to extend the life of our supplies."

"Yes, Miss Ria."

"Then I want you to gather the cleverest maidens in the tower and get them to work on plans. By tomorrow morning, I want three solid ideas on how to get everything of value in this tower outside of those walls."

"Right."

"Get another group to work at the mirrors. I need maidens contacting the leaders of other nations and notifying them about Magnus' behavior and our situation. They need to know our side of the story."

"I'm on it," Charise said. "Anything else?"

Ria halted and thought for a moment. "Tell everyone else to find ways to extend our ability to stay in this tower as long as we need to. If they can't think of anything, have them help someone who can."

"Will do," the girl confirmed with a nod. "Miss Ria, what are you going to do?"

"I'm going to find the finest craftsmen and a remote corner

of the world. We're building a new Aurora Tower."

20

The two-day journey home on the field-repaired Relentless seemed like the longest two days of Darius' life. Though he and Vasna had been elated to see the skyship gleaming in the light of the sunrise, their excitement had been short lived. The ship shuddered as pilots struggled to fly it back to Vatrisland with uneven thrust.

Over the course of the flight, Vasna went from limping, to being confined to a chair, to bed-bound, feverish and barely conscious. Darius barely slept as they travelled. For all of the fantastic power that the Titangavel had given him, his weapon had no answer for her condition. Every time he left Vasna's side over the course of those days, he clenched his fists in frustration. Both as Vatrisland's prince and as an Aurora Knight, he'd never felt so helpless in all of his life.

To make matters worse, the Oracle had told him of the standoff she was now locked in with his father.

"You must believe me, Darius," she'd pleaded. "This spy your father claims we harbor is a fabrication. It's an excuse to put Vatrisland's agents in Aurora Tower so that he can spy on us and intimidate us. He has no right!"

"Oracle, how do you know that there isn't a spy?"

She'd looked away. "I...I just know, Darius. You have to believe me on this."

She was hiding something. As soon as he'd finished speaking with her, he'd tried to contact his father via the ship's magic mirror, but couldn't get through.

"I'm sorry, Prince Darius," his father's speaker had said, "but King Magnus refuses to speak with you until he can do so face-to-face. He's made his feelings on the issue abundantly clear."

Considering the creature that had been released from the Cryptwastes, Darius hadn't exactly expected a parade to mark his return home, but this was something else entirely.

It had to be about Maxos. The past week had been so intense that he'd forgotten about defying his father's wishes. Vasna's slip of the tongue before they'd been cut off from each other had made him look that much more secretive.

Apology warred with anger inside him. He'd broken his word to his father, and that was something he had to own, but this wasn't the time. He didn't need another thing to worry about with Vasna's life at stake.

Now he watched Cloudbreach grow larger and larger from the front windows of The Relentless. Treve stood steady at the helm, but the dark circles under his eyes gave away his condition. He'd insisted on flying for longer shifts during the voyage home.

"I can make her go faster," he'd said each time they'd tried to relieve him.

No one had argued.

Darius called out to the Oracle and informed her of his impending arrival. She reassured him that, as he'd requested, she'd have Highbeacon, the radiant topaz-tipped spear, just inside the doors of Aurora Tower so that he could bind it to Vasna.

He left the bridge, made his way through the halls to the captain's quarters. Pierce was gently shutting the door as he arrived, and stopped when he spotted the prince. He'd borne Vasna's state with less composure than Treve, having taken it upon himself to make sure every need she'd expressed had been taken care of. More than a few times, he'd snapped at crewmen who'd been anything short of perfectly precise in handling her requests, but now he looked as though he run out of his former frantic energy.

"How's she doing?" Darius asked quietly as he approached.

Pierce just shook his head.

He clasped the shorter man's shoulder to reassure him. "I won't let her die, Pierce. I promise."

"I know you won't," Pierce replied. His voice was weak, but sincere.

He released Pierce's shoulder and the pilot walked off toward the bridge. Now alone, Darius pushed open the door to Vasna's room. Her state had so deteriorated that he'd stopped knocking before he entered. The few times she had been able to tell him it was okay to enter, her voice hadn't been loud enough to hear from outside the door anyway.

Vasna lay curled on her bed in the fetal position, half covered by a tangled mess of sheets, her skin as pale as snow. Her normally curly red hair had matted itself against her sweaty head, and she breathed in dry, hollow rasps. If she'd noticed Darius entering the room, she didn't show it.

The prince walked over to the bed and knelt beside her. "Vasna," he called out gently. "Hey, can you hear me?"

Her only reply was a weak, pained grunt. She contorted her face, as though the act of making a sound only hurt her further.

"Hold on, Vasna," he encouraged her. "We're almost there, okay? I'm gonna have to pick you up, and it might hurt a little, but we're gonna get you taken care of, okay?"

He'd hoped that asking questions would get some kind of response out of her that she was hearing or understanding him, but she didn't reassure him. To check on the wound, he tugged her loose shirt up just slightly. It had extended itself past her abdomen earlier, and just as it had every other time he'd checked on it, it had grown broader, darker, extending even more black tendrils across her skin. Sometimes he wondered why he worried himself checking on it anymore. It had looked worse every time, but he couldn't help but hope that maybe this time would be different.

"Okay, here we go," he told her, scooping her up as gently as he could. She winced weakly. Comforted that she was at least still moving, he carried her, stepping lightly through the halls of the ship and making his way. Before long, he reached the back of the skyship, and leaned against the wall to wait for the craft to touch down and lower the exit ramp.

"Darius?" She breathed out dryly in his arms.

He replied quickly. "Yeah, I'm here."

"When are you going to pick me up?" she asked.

Maybe she was going numb. He didn't want to think about what that might mean. There was no use explaining that to her. "In just a minute," he answered softly.

The hum of the crystals from outside of The Relentless grew louder. They had to be entering the hangar. Sure enough, seconds later, the vessel set down with a heavy clunk. Darius maneuvered his elbow to flip the lever controlling the ramp, and it slowly lowered.

Outside stood his father with crossed arms and a stony expression. Rows upon rows of Vatrisland's soldiers flanked him on either side. Each carried a shield in one hand and his unsheathed spellblade in the other. The adversarial display unnerved him. He'd never had his nation's own soldiers looking upon him with distrust before.

Darius walked slowly down the ship's ramp into the hangar, still cradling Vasna in his arms.

"Welcome home, son," his father said flatly.

"Father," he offered cautiously.

"We need to talk. Urgently," the king went on, businesslike in every word. "It seems we've had a misunderstanding."

"It has to wait. I need to take care of Vas—"

The king interrupted him forcefully. "We will talk now."

"No."

The word leapt from Darius' mouth before he even thought about it.

"No?" His father's unsettling calm began to slip away, revealing growing outrage. "Did you forget your position during your little excursion out to the Cryptwastes? How dare you defy me in public."

Magnus' rebuke twisted Darius' stomach into knots. A familiar reflex surged up. He'd failed his father. He needed to apologize. He shifted one foot backward and looked down to avoid eye contact as he responded. "W-what I mean is, father, I just really need to, to help her. She's wounded, but I can save her if I just give her one of the Aurora Arms."

"Drop her. She's dead to us."

Darius' snapped his head back up to judge his father's expression. The king's face was emotionless. "But, but she's done so much for us," he stammered back.

Magnus' calm returned. "Darius, if you make her one of your Knights, she'll have to leave Vatrisland to fight at your side. The kingdom will lose the finest mind the world of magecraft has ever known. If she dies, on the other hand, I lose her service as well, but it leaves us another weapon to put into the right hands."

The king paced his way across the hangar toward Darius as he continued, his cold, clicking footsteps echoing through the vast room. "This is your chance to redeem yourself for lying to me about the bow, boy. I will accept your apology if you give that spear to another general of my choosing; one with a suitable perspective on Vatrisland's importance relative to that of her neighbors."

Darius hesitated in his shock. Vasna had done so much to catapult their homeland to greatness, and had only given even greater service to help Vatrisland's troops out in the Cryptwastes. And now, to just dispose of her? Nausea swept over him as he tried to force out objections that refused to leave his mouth.

Magnus came to a stop right in front of him, speaking in a menacing whisper. "Do you know how much you disappointed me when you gave that weapon to the wrong man, Darius? You lied to me. You lied to your kingdom. You boarded my flagship as your own and then you spat in my face. Do you know what that makes you? You were no better than a thief to me. How lucky are you that I offer you a path to redemption now? Take it. I will not be so generous again."

Darius had no words. All over again, he was that small child, desperate to please his father. If he defied him now, there would be no turning back. He'd be outcast by the only family he had left.

"What will it be, Darius?" his father hissed. "Are you a good son? Are you my son?"

Darius clenched his teeth tightly and looked away. He still felt his father's expectant stare burrowing into him, inches away.

"Darius."

It was a whisper from Vasna, barely audible. He looked down at her. She was dying in his arms as he stood indecisive, succumbing to a wound she'd taken because she'd followed him into danger. She'd believed in him, and all it had earned her was a slow, agonizing death.

Just beyond the castle walls, the Oracle, Charise, and the shrine maidens awaited him in Aurora Tower. He hadn't been the Knight-Captain they'd expected, or even hoped for, but they'd pressed on, advised him, and encouraged him. They were waiting for him with Highbeacon at the ready to save Vasna.

Out somewhere between Vatrisland and H'tyanni territory, Maxos was pressing on alone, trying to stay one step ahead of a twelve story tall living disaster. The general had agreed to take on Watchward after Darius had unknowingly robbed him of the Titangavel. Even after Maxos had vented his frustrations, he'd reaffirmed his intent to make the best of things and fight on under his new destiny.

And in that moment, he knew his place.

"Father," he said quietly, "I will miss you."

With that, he stepped past his father and began to walk across the hangar.

At first, Darius heard no objection behind him. He thought perhaps he had stunned his father speechless. Then came the command. "Stop him."

The rows of soldiers standing between him and the hangar's exit moved to a ready position, their shields thrust out before them and spellblades raised high. Darius stopped and studied them. Though they kept their heads completely still, he could see their eyes darting back and forth in the shadows of their helmets, each trading glances with the soldiers beside him. He'd never seen Vatrisland's soldiers look so uncommitted to an order.

Vasna's breaths grew more faint.

"Do it. Stop me." Darius started again toward the soldiers.

They held position until the very last moment, but as he reached them cradling the limp captain in his arms, they lowered their blades and stepped aside for him, lowering their heads in deference. Darius walked the narrow aisle that formed for him and continued toward the door.

"I disown you today, Darius," his father stated, a slight air of sadness in his voice. "You will never sit upon Vatrisland's throne. You'll never again sleep in the room you called your own. And you will never, ever have my favor for the rest of your days."

Darius stopped and looked back across the room into his father's eyes. The most painful thing of all was that, try as he might, he couldn't tell whether his father was saddened to lose him, or at being defeated and humiliated.

His reply echoed across the quiet hangar. "You can't hurt me anymore. I deny you the power."

He didn't wait to see his father's response. Every word had been sincere. He reached the door and shouldered his way through.

XXX

As he approached Aurora Tower, Darius spotted Charise on a balcony high above the entrance. A wide smile spread across the girl's face, and she spun around quickly to yell something back into the tower. A moment later, the huge double doors swung open to reveal the entryway teeming with shrine maidens. At the center of the group stood the Oracle, cradling Highbeacon in her hands.

Darius passed through the threshold, and the maidens behind him quickly resealed the door. He laid Vasna's limp form on the ground before the Oracle. When he looked up, she was holding the spear out for him.

"I'm sure this isn't how you'd prefer I pick my Knights," Darius began.

"I trust you." Her response was immediate. Not a moment of hesitation. She still held the spear out for him in open hands.

Darius nodded. He took the shining spear from the Oracle and curled Vasna's limp fingers around its haft. "Vasna Hain," he declared, "as the Knight-Captain of the Aurora Knights, I hereby bind to you Highbeacon, Herald of Brilliance. Take up this weapon and defend the world in the face of its most desperate hour. As of this day, you are an Aurora Knight."

The weapon sparked to life with golden fire. The blaze coursed up Vasna's arms, illuminating her from head to toe. She gasped, opening her eyes wide as the weapon's power suffused her. Through the near-blinding glare, Darius could see the vile, black wound receding down her abdomen. It shrank back further and further until it vanished entirely. So far as he could see, it didn't even leave a scar behind.

The great blaze dimmed away to reveal Vasna's face, tears

of joy streaming down her cheeks as she gasped in excited breaths. The crowd of maidens burst into an elated cheer as Darius drew her into his arms and held her.

21

The next morning, Ria stood before one of the magic mirrors within Aurora Tower's vault with Darius and Vasna behind her on either side. Maxos looked back at the three from the mirror's surface with a grim frown, and though the topic at hand was serious, having her current three Knights all before her at once filled her with hope and vigor.

"Fort Diligence was devastated," Maxos reported. "I ran into a few soldiers who'd scattered away from the fort before the beast had reached it. They said Hrax didn't even need to get within range of the siege weapons. He spit a white beam of light that vaporized the walls, dumping all of the mounted cannons into the drill yard. Then he was on the fort clawing and eating before they could recover. Those who stayed to fight never had a chance."

Ria winced. The soldiers at the fort had stood no chance against Hrax, but it didn't soften the blow of the very news she'd expected. The Harbinger of Ruin had devoured not just thousands of Vatrisland's men, but if the legends were true, their very essences as well. Every spirit he'd consumed would increase his power further. "What about you, Maxos?" she asked him. "Where are you? Are you safe?"

The former general nodded. "I've taken shelter with the men I ran into at the last station outside the H'tyanni border. With any luck, I'll be at Aksa'ol in two days, maybe three. From there, well...."

"Brace for impact?" Darius offered.

Maxos nodded reluctantly. "I wish I could say I had a better plan, but we're talking hundreds of thousands of people. It's not a number that we could hide or relocate, so until all of the Aurora Arms are bound to Knights, we're going to have to mount the best defense we can muster, and pray."

"We'll get to you as quickly as we can," Vasna reassured him, before adding with a hint of bitterness, "It's a shame we won't have The Relentless at our disposal, but as we explained, one of us did sort of burn that bridge to ash and cinders." She eyed Darius.

"I mentioned that he told me to let you die, right?" he began.

"I know, I know," she answered with a sigh. "I just hate to lose my baby like this."

Ria half-smiled. They were already bonding. "I know this isn't going to sound particularly comforting, but get used to setbacks. We don't assemble a team of Aurora Knights to deal with things anyone else could have solved, and the more constructive you can be in the face of adversity, the better you'll do both for one another, and for the innocents you'll help."

The Knights all paused for a moment before Darius confirmed, "That's true, actually. I've working with her the longest of all of us, and that really is the least comforting thing she's said since I joined up."

Maxos and Vasna grinned quietly, shaking their heads. Ria smiled at them all despite herself, pleased that their spirits were high enough that they could joke. "Never tell anyone that I sugarcoated it for you then," she added with a smirk.

"Well, do your best to haul out here as soon as possible, you two," Maxos encouraged them. "I'll need as much support as I can get in Aksa'ol. And don't forget, Darius; you've got a potential Knight to meet when you get there."

"Sounds like a plan," Darius agreed. "Who is she,

220

anyway?"

"Are any of you familiar with Tanta Chuus?"

Ria looked at Darius and Vasna in turn. They each looked as stumped as she was.

"What if I tell you that it means Racing Breeze in H'tyanni?"

Ria lit up. "The masked vigilante?"

"The very same," Maxos confirmed. "We crossed paths when I chased some thieves out of a tea house during a visit with my wife's family. She's got the spirit of a Knight for sure. The H'tyanni people adore her, and for good reason."

Ria nodded in agreement. "If even half of her legend is true, she'll make a wonderful recruit. I've heard she passes on the coin she seizes from breaking criminal dealings to the poor and needy if she can't find a rightful owner."

Vasna and Darius both nodded approvingly.

"I'm glad you like her so far. She won't disappoint you when you meet her," Maxos said confidently. "But enough talk for now. I'll get on the road. Be safe, friends." His face faded from the magic mirror.

Ria and the two remaining Knights walked over to the statues that held the unassigned Aurora Arms. Freestar and Feygrip glittered in the morning sunlight. Darius and Vasna each took one and bundled it in a thick cloth that Ria had provided.

As the three looked over the Knights' supplies for the journey one last time, Darius piped up. "I really don't like the idea of leaving you and the maidens here at the tower the way things are with my father now. Are you sure you'll all be okay here?"

Ria sighed. "Honestly, no. The need for you in Aksa'ol is far too great to keep one of you behind though, so we'll manage for now. This place has been our bastion for nearly a thousand years now, and I hate to leave it behind after all that's been done to ward and protect it, but the climate here has indeed grown hostile.

I've begun serious research into having a new tower built."

Vasna offered some hope. "If you think you can do so without gathering attention, talk to my assistants, Pierce and Treve. I give you my word they're more loyal to me than they are to the crown. After what King Magnus said about me yesterday, I think you'll find their expertise remarkably helpful."

"Thank you, Vasna," Ria told her with a warm smile. Already, their growing numbers were offering her contacts to aid the Knights' cause that she couldn't have hoped to arrange on her own. Darius' decision to offer Vasna one of the Aurora Arms hadn't just been mercy. The young woman would make a fine Knight.

The thought caused her to look the young Knight-Captain over. He'd come so far in only a week. Faced with an intense trial-by-fire, he'd risen to the occasion admirably. He seemed less afraid to own his decisions, even controversial ones.

"Well, if that's everything, time's wasting," Darius told her. "Want to come down and see us off at the doors?"

"I would love to," she said, beaming back at her Knights.

Darius and Vasna gathered their belongings, and together all three of them rode the lift down to the base of Aurora Tower. The great doors groaned open, letting in a brisk spring breeze as they revealed the castle grounds beneath a cloudless sky.

"Have you arranged transportation for the journey?" Ria asked them.

Vasna answered first. "My personal hound was stabled outside of the castle walls. I'll be getting a hold of her on the way out of the city."

"And I got Comet outside of the city walls yesterday before father's formal blacklisting kicked in," Darius said, referring to his own hound. "Truth be told, we haven't ridden together in so long that he probably doesn't even know I have the old mutt, but better safe, I figured."

"Indeed," Ria replied. "Ride swiftly then, Aurora Knights. The maidens and I will contact you as the situation progresses here. Know that we're here for you. Do not hesitate to ask us for anything."

The two nodded and began to walk out before Darius halted, putting out an arm to stop Vasna beside him. He turned back to Ria once more. "You know, Maxos did tell me that he was meant to be Knight-Captain before my father came along and turned things upside down on you. Why didn't you warn me about that?"

Ria responded, "If you'd have known what he was meant for, you'd never have judged him on your own. It happened this way so that you'd never have to second guess your decision to make him a Knight."

"And if I had picked Andler instead?"

"That whole situation did worry me at first, I'll grant you," she confessed. "But when I thought about who you were and what you valued, let go and left it in your hands. You have more wisdom than you credit yourself for."

Darius nodded. "Well," he went on, "I still don't feel right about taking this position away from him. Especially considering what's gone on between me and my father at this point."

He looked right into Ria's eyes and went on sincerely. "So even though the Titangavel is mine, as of today, I'm considering it on loan to me."

She cocked her head to one side. "What does that mean?"

"My father gave me something I didn't deserve. It's too late for me to earn this weapon now, since I already have it, but I'm going to use it like I could have it taken away and given to someone else. I'm not the right man to carry it yet. I still have a lot to learn. But, when I'm done, there won't be any question that I've earned it,"

She couldn't help but laugh happily. Darius had a different

way of thinking about things. She found herself thanking the stars that such an initially frightening twist of fate had placed him in her life. "Very well," she answered, "I accept your terms."

Darius grinned and nodded at her one last time, and with that, the two Knights strode off toward the eastern horizon to face down Hrax, the Harbinger of Ruin.

26257870R00127

Made in the USA
Charleston, SC
30 January 2014